THE BOY IN THE BURNING HOUSE

TIM WYNNE-JONES

THE BOY IN THE BURNING HOUSE

A NOVEL

A GROUNDWOOD BOOK
DOUGLAS & McINTYRE
TORONTO VANCOUVER

The author is grateful for the generous support of the
Canada Council for the Arts
towards the writing of this book.

Copyright © 2000 by Tim Wynne-Jones
Fourth printing 2001

Groundwood Books/Douglas & McIntyre
720 Bathurst Street, Suite 500
Toronto, Ontario M5S 2R4

We acknowledge the financial support of the Canada Council for the Arts, the
Ontario Arts Council and the Government of Canada through the Book
Publishing Industry Development Program for our publishing activities.

Canadian Cataloguing in Publication Data

Wynne-Jones, Tim
The boy in the burning house
A Groundwood book.
ISBN 0-88899-410-9
I. Title.
PS8595.Y59B69 2000   jC813'.54   C00-931030-4
PZ7.W993Bo 2000

Design by Michael Solomon
Cover illustration by Greg Spalenka (www.spalenka.com)
Printed and bound in Canada

ACKNOWLEDGEMENTS

This novel grew out of a short story called "The Bermuda Triangle," which appeared in my collection *Lord of the Fries*. I am thankful to Melanie Kroupa for suggesting that I think about following up on the unsolved mystery that is at the heart of that short story.

The novel gathered momentum thanks to an article in the archives of the *Perth Courier*. I would like to thank John Clement and Maureen Pegg and the staff there for letting me poke around the old volumes at my leisure.

A writer is always in debt to good librarians, and Perth is blessed with two of the best: Faye Cunningham and Susan Snyder, thanks. But also, in this case, I'd like to thank the resourceful Ann MacPhail at Algonquin College. Dave Onion proved helpful at one critical point in the story, as did David Sentesy. Thank you, gentlemen.

And thank you to my family: Amanda, Xan, Maddy and Lewis, who continue to put up with me. Stories come and go; thank God for family.

Readers lucky enough to know Perth and its eastern Ontario environs may notice a similarity to the town of Ladybank and North Blandford Township, the fictional setting of this story. That passing resemblance does not, however, extend to the characters, all of whom are completely fictional. I have certainly never met nor heard tell of a man quite like Father Fisher. Certainly not in these parts.

This book is for Magdalene
with love and admiration

To dig or not to dig, that is the question.
From *The Prospectors' Soliloquy*

In a windowless room off the kitchen hallway, Father Fisher did his praying. It had once been a pantry but there was no food in it anymore, just food for thought. That's what Father liked to say. Ruth Rose couldn't care less about his religious books, his tracts, the Acts and Epistles of the Apostles. The letters she was after weren't so high-minded.

Somebody was trying to blackmail Father.

She wasn't a complete fool, no matter what anybody said. She didn't expect it would be easy to find proof and no one was going to believe her without it. So she searched when and where she could, and watched and listened.

It was after midnight. She sat in the broom closet. The closet smelled of vinegar and detergent, of Windex and Pledge. She had the door open a crack. Street light sifted through the back door window. She rocked back and forth, concentrating.

He was in there, across the narrow hall, in his own darkness.

He hadn't shut the door all the way. She could hear the old oak prayer-stall creak under his weight. How penitent he sounded, with his God this and God that. "I have sinned," he said. "I come before you, O, God, with a heavy heart," he said. "Empty me, O, Lord," he said. "Lighten me."

He mumbled, snuffled a bit. She tuned him in like a night radio station transmitting from a long way off. His voice, pulpit-tempered and sermon-strong, quivered and quavered around the edges. He was agitated, whining. Good.

"Take me back," he said. His voice became trance-like. Praying did that to him, sometimes. She had watched him sway in church as if under a spell, but that was mostly holy show for the congregation. It was only in the praying room that he gave voice to his deeper secrets. They crawled out of the cave of his mouth in whispers and groans.

"Help me..."

His voice cracked, changed. Ruth Rose held her breath.

"Tabor, can you keep a secret?"

It was not his voice. Somewhere down inside his massive frame, Father had dug up the voice of a boy.

"Pssst!" he hissed, and the sizzle of it made Ruth Rose jerk her head backwards, hitting the shelf above her. A toilet roll fell onto her lap, then bounced onto the floor, bumping against a washing pail. She swallowed a yelp. Then, grabbing a broom, she readied to fight her way out if need be. Had she roused him from his trance? Was he alert now at the other end of this rope of silence, ready to tug her out of hiding?

He spoke again. "You all right?" he whispered.

Ruth Rose rubbed the sore spot on the back of her head. No, she wanted to answer. But he wasn't talking to her.

"It opens up farther along," he said. "Come on. Hoof it, guys!"

There was an urgency to his voice. He called out. "Tuffy? Tuffy, you in there?"

Ruth Rose rocked, soaking up the whispers, her eyes squeezed shut. She knew some of this cast of characters by name only. Tabor, Tuffy, Laverne — she had no idea who they were. Then there was Hub. Hub who was dead now.

Father cleared his throat, startling her again. Her foot had gone to sleep, her head ached, the smell of the closet nauseated her. There had to be a better way.

She needed help. She frowned to herself in the dark, her fists clenched on her knees so hard her black fingernails left halfmoon wounds in her palms. She hated the idea of asking anyone for help. But there *was* someone. If she could just get him to listen.

1

From the school bus Jim Hawkins caught sight of the flooded land. The bus was trundling up the cut road.

There were just the two of them: Everett behind the wheel humming a Prairie Oyster tune and Jim at his usual station, halfway back, nose pressed against the window. Not that he was looking for anything; it was just his way of staying far enough from Eager Everett to avoid a conversation.

That was how he noticed the glitter of light on water where there shouldn't have been any.

The cut road followed the eastern property line of the Hawkins land. It was mostly mixed hardwood down that end, but there was swamp land, fed by a creek. Incognito Creek, his father had called it, because it didn't draw much attention to itself, didn't gurgle or splash much. Kind of like Jim himself.

But no stream, however insignificant, could avoid the detection of a beaver looking to start a home. The flood Jim had glimpsed was in a gulch where his father had cut a trail to a high grazing area at the southeast corner of the farm. The pasture was only a few acres but it would be lost to them if the beavers took the gulch. It wouldn't be the first time they had tried. It was a natural depression, narrow necked and easy to dam.

"Podner, we gotta clear the pass of them varmints," his father used to say, putting on his idea of a cowboy drawl.

Jim pressed his forehead hard against the cool glass of the bus window. He wasn't sure he could handle varmints alone.

He and his mother didn't need the southeast pasture all that much, he tried to tell himself. They'd sold off the beef cattle; could barely keep up with the few head of dairy they still had. But losing his father had been bad enough. He wasn't about to see the land stolen out from under them. It had been Hawkins land for five generations. Hadn't his father said that enough times?

The cut road came to a T-intersection at the Twelfth Line, and Everett turned west. Jim gathered up his stuff and made his way down the aisle. Everett caught his eye.

"Corn lookin' good there, Jimbo. No blight. Lar Perkins, he's got the blight. And him with his bum knee. No Geritol hockey for him this season, eh."

Eager Everett. Eye contact was all it took to flip his switch. Jim smiled in a polite way, and the bus pulled to a stop at his driveway. Everett cranked open the doors.

"My best to your mother," he said, tipping his Blue Jays baseball cap. He was like a jay himself once he got squawking.

The bus rumbled on up the Twelfth until it was swallowed in its own dust. Jim stood at the end of his driveway swallowed up by a memory. His father waiting right here for him with a pickaxe in one meaty hand and a long-handled spade in the other.

"You up for some counterinsurgency manoeuvres,

son?" Not cowboys this time but some kind of SWAT team.

Jim had slipped off his backpack right away. "The beavers again, huh?"

His father had nodded. "Let's take 'em out, Jimbo."

It had been a day not unlike this, early fall. The year before his father vanished.

Jim crossed the yard and opened the back door before his mother's shout caught up with him. He looked over towards the driveshed. She was standing in the doorway in coveralls and rubber boots, with a baseball cap on backwards and a paper mask pulled down under her chin. She held a spray can in her hand.

She made her way towards him across the yard. Behind her in the shadows of the shed stood his father's car, a '65 Chevy Malibu, Yuma yellow. She was touching up the bodywork. She was going to sell it. Had to.

Snoot, their six-month-old kitten, darted out the open kitchen door through Jim's legs. He swept her up into his arms, watched his mother draw closer, saw her smile through the tiredness on her face. She was working the night shift at the factory. She clomped up onto the porch, made as if to spray him with the primer. He held up the kitten in defence. They laughed. Then he handed Snoot to her, kicked off his shoes and stepped into his rubber boots. She held the kitten like a baby, stroking her dove-grey stomach.

"Where you headed?" she asked.

"Beavers have taken the pass," he said, trying to sound jokey and gruff.

"Want a hand?"

Jim shook his head. "I'll take Gladys. That okay?"

His mother smiled. "Oh, I'm sure she'll appreciate it. Doesn't get much company these days."

Jim plonked back down the steps to the yard. "Everett sends his best," he said without turning. He had to pass on the message, but he didn't like it. Didn't like men paying attention to his mother.

"Why, I think I'll just phone him right up and ask him over for corn and potato chowder," she said in a jaunty voice. She posed like a fashion model, glamorous in her black overalls and ball cap, her face freckled with red primer paint. "What's the use of getting all dolled up if there aren't any gentlemen callers," she added, batting her eyelashes.

Jim managed a chuckle despite himself.

Gladys stood a little worse for wear in the garden. The garden didn't need a scarecrow anymore. It was fall-weary, mostly dead but for the pumpkins and carrots. There were still withered scarlet runners clinging like arthritic fingers to the vine, winter squash, a few behemoth zucchini — nothing any bird was about to carry off.

The scarecrow wore a stained and decrepit white tux, a purple fedora and a pink fright-wig glued to a semi-deflated volleyball head.

"Hmmm," said Jim, looking her over. "I'm trying to imagine a beaver frightened enough of you to fly away." Gladys just grinned.

With the scarecrow on his shoulder and a shovel in his free hand, Jim walked along the tractor lane through the cornfield. Arnold Tysick and Ormond McCoy from up the line towards Onion Station had helped them plant the corn that spring and had already volunteered to help with the harvest. There hadn't been a frost yet, but it wouldn't be long. It took two or three good hard frosts to dry out the feed corn just right.

Jim was trying to remember stuff like that now. He had helped with the farm work since he was six or so, but he was going to have to pay special attention from now on. In the summer, his mother had found work at the Jergens soap factory in Ladybank. Money was tight. They weren't sure what they were going to do about the farm. Hold on as best they could, for the time being. There was no way Iris Hawkins would hear of Jim dropping out of school.

"What would Hub have thought of that?" she had said to him. His father never finished grade eleven, but he regretted it all his life and made up for it as best he could. He had been an avid reader, mostly history.

"How're you gonna know what to do if you don't know what you did?" he used to say. And sometimes he would add in a mocking, grave tone, "Jimbo, history is all we've got in this God-forsaken corner of the county."

Jim placed Gladys's gloved hand on his left shoulder and whirled around as if they were dancing. An odd couple — he in gumboots and overalls, Gladys's tux tails flapping in the bright fall air. He'd seen his dad dance with Gladys.

The memories came on like this sometimes, like a sweet, sad avalanche. He had learned to ride them out, not to fight them. But there had been a time when the memories had come on so fiercely that they stopped up his throat so he could hardly breathe. For three months he hadn't been able to talk. Not a word. Only bit by bit did he get his voice back, his life back. But not Hub.

Crossing the stile into the lower meadow, Gladys's head fell off.

"Can't take you anywhere," said Jim, leaning the scarecrow torso against the fence. He rescued the volleyball head from the weedy overgrowth, getting a handful of prickles for his troubles.

As he sat on the stile sucking out the pain, he noticed a Coke can in the long grass. It looked new. He picked it up, looked around. It was too early in the season for hunters. He squashed the can under his boot. Then, having nowhere else to put it, shoved it through the neck hole into Gladys's head. There was nothing much else in there but rags and pebbles and a few dead moths. He plumped the head back onto her broom-handle neck. It rattled.

He ploughed on, getting more and more worked up. He didn't like to think of people trespassing on the farm, didn't like the idea of strangers sneaking around.

He stumbled on down the tractor trail into the woodland that separated the cornfields from the low swampy area. He stopped at the threshold of a shadowy place where the woods closed in tight on the road, forming a canopy that blocked the light.

This was the spot. This was where they found his car.

Jim took a deep breath, let it out slowly. His lungs filled with the heavy fragrance of cedar.

The cops found nothing. No signs of a fight. No cigarette butts, no threads — just Dad's old Malibu, the first car he had ever bought, the keys in the ignition. Outside there was a footprint or two in the muck. They came from a pair of boots Dad always wore. Matched up exactly with footprints in the barnyard.

After the initial search, volunteers came in droves to help out. Someone found a little tube of lip balm up towards the railway tracks and everyone went crazy as if they'd found a map or something. But it belonged to one of the volunteers who'd combed that part of the woods already. Then, at the fence, they found a tiny fragment of yarn hanging from a barb. The colour matched a sweater Hub had put on that morning. In the swamp land beyond the tracks, they found more of the footprints and, finally, a mile south of the farm, at a water-filled quarry, they found one of his blue handkerchiefs. They dragged the quarry but found no body.

It was as if Hub Hawkins had been spirited away. It was as if God had dropped down in a spacecraft and whisked him off the face of the earth. "Hey, Hub, we've got big beaver problems in heaven. The angels are getting the skirts of their robes wet. We could use some first-hand advice."

Jim smiled, but the smile died on him. It was harder and harder to believe his father might somehow, somewhere, still be alive. Jim remembered the tracker dogs, the choppers, the experts from Toronto, the press.

He looked up as hard and high as he could, but he saw no heaven, no angels with wet skirts. No God.

Gladys's head fell off again. He stooped to pick it up. "You know what I think, Gladys? I think you're kind of like God," he said. "Something we made up to scare off the crows."

After the authorities had given up, Jim came down here, insane with longing, cursing everyone and everything. He came again and again. Fighting back the fear of what he might find or what might find him.

It was in this cedar glade that he lost his voice. He had been looking around, hoping beyond hope he might spot some clue everyone had overlooked. He had gone to call out his father's name — only nothing came out of his mouth.

He stopped coming. It had always been a favourite cross-country ski trail. He and his mother found other trails, not that they got out much last winter. In the summer, Lar Perkins came through with his bush hog to keep the trail passable. Never asked to be paid. But Jim never came down this way again. Not until today.

"What do ya think, Gladys?" he said. He waggled her head up and down and heard the Coke can rattle. The sound fired him up again. Then he stepped into the shadows of the glade and passed through to the light on the other side.

Before he saw the beaver pond he was walking in it. The road was squelchy wet even though it hadn't rained for days. He rounded a curve in the rutted lane and there it was, as wide across as a football field and stretching out of sight into the alder scrub on one side and the poplar woods on the other.

A beaver emerged from the far undergrowth dragging a branch. Jim watched it for a moment. Quietly leaning Gladys against a tree, he raised the business end of the shovel to his shoulder as if it were a rifle.

"Bang!"

With a loud slap of its tail the beaver vanished underwater. Jim pretended to blow the smoke off the mouth of the barrel.

"Take that, you lousy varmint," he said. Then he headed around the edge of the pond through the submerged grass towards the dam site.

He knew whatever he did today wouldn't be enough. The beavers would be back. It was like a hockey game, his father used to say. The fourth period would be sudden death.

Mud sucking at his boot heels, Jim clambered to the top of the dam and started in chopping at the lattice-work of branches and sticks that constituted this latest instalment of Hawkins against Nature. The dam was wattle and daub: mud interwoven with grass, weeds and supple willow canes that made the wall hard to tear apart. Putting his back into it, Jim lifted a shovel load that came up with a great sucking sound and the stench of rotten vegetation. The dammed water rushed through the breach.

He worked for a good twenty minutes without stopping. The air was still warm but the wind was freshening. The dry leaves overhead shimmered, gold-edged and dying. There was no sound but the prattle of blue jays, the squelch of muck and, loudest of all, the water gushing and splashing over his feet.

Jim straightened up, out of breath. Gladys was watching him from her resting place against a sapling birch.

There was a noise in the woods. Jim turned to look. A moment passed before a squirrel appeared on a dead log and scolded him. A hawk circled overhead, screeching. Jim craned his neck.

The racing water slowed to a trickle. He had done a pretty good job. He wasn't sure how much more he could do. The big thing had been getting here at all.

He leaned on his shovel, sniffed the air — a great big lung-filling sniff.

"Ah, corn and potato chowder," he said. It was the

kind of thing his father would have said. A set-up for Jimbo. "Funny, all I smell is beaver poop."

Jim sloshed his way through the cloudy remains of the pond to dry land and Gladys. He patted her on the shoulder.

"Glad," he said. "You did such a good job this summer, you got a promotion. We want you to keep the beavers from fixing up this here dam. You think you can handle it?" Gladys wobbled her head, nodding. "Good for you," he said. Then he picked up the scarecrow and waded back to the hole in the dam. He drove her broom-handle base down into the mud, twisting it until she stood firmly in place. Then he took a step back and looked solemnly at her grinning mug.

"Now, here's the gross part," he said. "Beavers don't see so well. So — and I don't want you to take this personal — the only way we're going to keep those beavers away is if you smell bad. Bad as a human being."

Gladys stared dumbly at him. He felt dumb, too — talking to a scarecrow. He remembered the first time his dad told him they were going to pee on the scarecrow.

"And that would be because we're perverts?" Jim had said.

His father had laughed. "Not so. To a beaver, human beings stink to high heaven. Eau de wee-wee is the answer. They'll be wary of coming too close."

Like wolves, thought Jim, staking out their territory. Then, without further ado, he opened his zipper and let fly.

There was another disturbance in the woods while he stood there baptizing Gladys. Another squirrel, he thought, as his eyes travelled to the source of the noise.

But what he saw there wasn't an animal — not a small one, at least. He caught a glimpse of black hair, a flash of pale skin. Enough to be certain that what he saw was a girl.

2

There was the initial shock, and then a moment of bottom-of-the-barrel humiliation followed by an adrenaline rush of blinding rage. Like a rocket, Jim exploded out of the muck, charging over the dam towards the woods, pulling up his zipper as he ran and yelling his head off. The girl had a good head start on him and she was wearing sneakers, not gumboots, but even though he fell a couple of times, slipping in the mud, tripping over branches, something drove him on with a will and he stayed with her.

It wasn't just the shame of being caught like that. It was something else. A grudge. Unfinished business with the forest. And there was more. She was laughing at him. Laughing like a crazy person!

He chased the girl through face-slapping firs, down muddy deer paths, across rocky mounds and over a rotting split-rail fence. He chased her along Incognito Creek and then scrabbled up the steep wooded slope to the back meadow, catching glimpses of her but never catching up to her.

And then she was gone. He was on the high meadow now and she was nowhere to be seen.

He heard a train coming. Standing up to his waist in the tall grass, as still as a scarecrow, he watched it pass, a slow freight. From where he stood he saw only the rusty tops of the cars. Then it was gone, rattling its way southeast towards Ladybank. He strode to the fence line and peered down the embankment to the tracks. She wasn't hiding there.

He whirled around, as if maybe she was lying low or creeping up on him. He cupped his hands.

"This is private property," he yelled at the wild field. "Don't come round here!" His words echoed off the wall of dark woods that surrounded the field. Big-man words in a high-pitched kid's voice. He listened for laughter, heard nothing but the distant clatter of the train.

Then he heard a dog.

The barking came from up the tracks. It sounded ferocious. Scared stiff, Jim swore under his breath, wishing he'd kept his angry outburst bottled up. Once in a while, wild dog packs came around, more dangerous than wolves. Berserk. They would kill cattle just for the fun of it.

But as the barking came nearer, Jim realized it was only one dog, and as it came nearer still, he recognized its voice.

The cornfield dog — that's what he called it — coming up the tracks like a noisy caboose trying to catch the train. Then it veered up the embankment from the railroad bed, shinnying under the fence — a lab retriever with a pelt the colour of corn husks, shaggy and uncombed, full of twigs and burrs. It came straight for him and ran around him like a dirty blond whirlwind, barking up a storm.

"Cut it out," said Jim. "Shut up, you stupid mutt."

The dog sat, but its body wriggled with excitement and its mouth lolled open. It wore a collar but Jim had no idea who it belonged to. It showed up sometimes when he was out on the land, always with this eager look on its face, as if anything you might be up to would be more interesting than sitting around the farmyard watching laundry dry.

"Whoa, boy," said Jim, calmly now. He reached out to scratch the dog's head, but it suddenly tore off again before he could lay a hand on it. It stopped over by the woods to see if he was coming.

"I don't have time for games," Jim shouted. The sun was already nearing the tree line and he didn't plan on walking back through the woods in the dark.

But the dog barked again and raced towards a towering pine tree right on the property line. The dog stood at the base of the tree, four-square, looking up, barking for all it was worth, its tail wagging hard enough to start a brush fire. And following its gaze, Jim saw the girl, all in black, perched like a crow on a branch, scowling down at him.

Jim ran over to join the dog. "Good boy," he said. "Good dog."

The next thing he knew, a pine cone hit him on the head. It was followed by a cascade of laughter and more pine cones.

Jim stepped back, covering his head. When he was out of range, he looked up and cupped his hands.

"You can laugh all you want," he shouted. "But my dog here is a killer."

The girl laughed so hard she almost lost her grip.

"That dog's name is Poochie," she shouted down to him. "Poochie's Bryce Hoover's dog and he couldn't kill an apple."

Poochie barked at Jim, a big doggie grin on his face as if he had been in on the joke all along.

Then the girl slithered down the tree. She swung

out in an arc from a branch above Jim's head and landed like an acrobat before him. He backed off, but then he recognized her.

"You're the pastor's daughter," he said.

"Wrooooong!"

Poochie had gone to her and she scruffled his neck feathers with long pale fingers, the bitten nails painted black. The dog smiled up at her, drooling like a fool.

"You are so," said Jim. "Father Fisher's kid. I remember seeing you in church."

She snarled. "I haven't been to church in three years."

Jim didn't say anything, unsure all of a sudden. It had been most of a year since he had been to church himself. Didn't see much point in it anymore.

He stared at the girl. He could be wrong. If it was her, she had changed, got herself some breasts and an attitude. She was all in black from her sneakers to her dark-and-stormy-night hair. It was inky black, from a bottle, he guessed. Even her lips were black. She had a gold nose ring. She looked tough as nails. And yet there was something sweet — a scent of roses — which was how he remembered her name.

"Ruth Rose," he said.

"Bzzzz!" she buzzed like a bee. "A hundred points for Jim Hawkins who pisses on scarecrows."

Jim grabbed at her but she danced back out of his way.

"Give it up," she said. "You couldn't catch me if you tried. You only found me because I wanted to be found." There was something about the way she said it that made Jim realize it was the truth. "You've done a fair share of tree climbing yourself," she said with a snarky smile. Jim went cold all over.

Suddenly, Poochie tore off towards the tracks. They watched him go. When he was out of sight, Jim tried to change the subject.

"You don't live around here," he said.

Ruth Rose shoved her hands into the back pockets of her jeans and jutted out her chin. "See that railroad? That's my home. Ruth Rose Way. I own that railroad. I know every farm, every gravel lot, every lumber yard that backs onto that track all the way to Ladybank."

"So?"

"So I know everything. Like about you, for instance."

"Big deal."

She smiled slyly. "Mr. Tarzan," she said. "I saw you out here leaping from tree to tree like a maniac ape."

Jim looked down.

"I saw you climbing to the top and whipping the tree back and forth and then jumping — WHEEEEEEEE!" She waggled her arms around in free fall. She paused and when she spoke again her voice was low and almost tender. "Trying to kill yourself, would be my guess," she said. "I know all about that."

There was a hook in the last sentence that dragged Jim's chin up off his chest.

"Why don't you just tell me what you're doing here," he said. He saw something like doubt flit across her eyes, as if she had known exactly what she was doing until this very moment. She pushed her hair back, put her hands on her hips, looked away towards the tracks, as if maybe, like Poochie, she was going to bolt.

"Listen," said Jim impatiently. "My mom goes to work soon and I gotta be home."

"She doesn't leave 'til nine," said Ruth Rose.

"This is creepy," said Jim. "Why are you spying on us?"

"Because I've been checking you out," she said.

Jim had known one crazy person in his life, Billy Bones. On the few occasions Jim had been close enough to look into Billy's eyes, he'd seen a kind of looseness of focus, as if Billy couldn't hold onto where his thoughts were going to take him next, and his eyes had the devil of a job just to keep up.

Jim looked into Ruth Rose's eyes — moss green they were — to see if she was crazy, too. She stared right back at him without a flicker. Maybe there were different kinds of craziness.

"I'm here," she said, "because of that Fisher-man. He may have married my mother, but he will never be my father. If we're going to work together you'd better get that through your tweenie skull."

"Work together?"

"Just listen!" she said. Her hands had curled into fists, and Jim didn't doubt she would use them. He swallowed, listened.

"Fisher is a murderer," she said.

Jim snapped his head back as if, with a lightning sucker punch, she *had* hit him.

"What?"

"You heard me." Her voice was all breathy now. She looked around as if Father Fisher might be in the field somewhere. Then she returned her gaze to Jim, her green eyes flashing. "And you're going to help me put him away."

It was obvious now she *was* crazy. Jim shook his head in disbelief and turned to go.

"Don't move," she said. Jim froze. She walked

around him, blocking his path. She was a head taller than he was and bristling with wiry strength.

"That's better," she said. She blew the hair off her face. "You don't really know anything about him. You probably don't even know that his name actually is Father. Even my mom calls him Father, which is gross."

Jim tried to speak as gently as he could, not wanting to disturb her any more than she already was.

"I'm sorry," he said. "But this doesn't have anything to do with me."

She went on as if she hadn't heard. "When he became a pastor, he got his name legally changed to Father. He used to be Eldon, Eldon Fisher. Do you know what a fisher is?"

"Like Christ, a fisher of souls — "

"Wroooong! I mean the animal."

"Like a weasel," said Jim.

"Worse," said Ruth Rose. "More like a wolverine."

"Yeah." Jim had seen a fisher that a trapper caught. And he remembered what the trapper had called it. "A killing machine," he said.

Ruth Rose nodded appreciatively. "Do you know how a fisher kills a porcupine, Jim? It hides up in the tree where the porcupine lives and when the porkie comes home in the morning and heads out to its branch to sleep, the fisher drops down in front of it from the branch above. The porcupine can't turn around — the branch is too small — so it can't defend itself with its tail. And then do you know what?" She stepped right up to Jim as if she were the fisher and he were the porcupine. "The fisher bites the porcupine's face off."

Jim tensed. Then he relaxed a bit and rolled his eyes.

"You think I'm an idiot, don't you?" she said. "Go on, say it."

"You're an idiot," said Jim. Then she shoved him so hard he tumbled right over and before he could move she was standing over him.

"He got his name changed to Father, all legal and everything. Just like he legally adopted me when he married my mom. He likes to make things look neat and tidy. You know why? Because he's got a lot to hide."

Jim flinched. September nights came on quickly and here he was, far from home, gabbing with a lunatic.

"I've got to go," he said, edging upwards to a sitting position. When she didn't pounce, he clambered to his feet.

"Don't you want to hear who he murdered?" she said.

Jim shook his head. "No, thank you." He started walking away, didn't look back.

"I'll tell your mother," she shouted after him. "About your tree jumping." He didn't stop. Those days were behind him.

"I need your help, Jim," she said.

"You need somebody's help," he muttered to himself. He glanced back to see if she'd heard. He had only walked twenty paces or so, but he could hardly see her. In her black clothing, she was lost in the shadow of the pine tree. Now that he had opened some distance between them, he felt a little sorry for her.

"I'm sorry I can't help," he shouted.

"You will be," she hollered back at him.

He shuddered at the fury in her voice, but was far enough away by now to laugh to himself at her threat.

He was heading down the hill towards the creek

which flowed by as sly as a rumour, when she called out to him again. He looked up and she was standing above him at the lip of the hill, silhouetted against the light — dark and mysterious like a cut-out.

"Jim Hawkins," she shouted, trying to catch her breath. "Fisher killed your father."

3

He wanted to hit her. "Shut up," he said.
"I don't know how to shut up," she said,
advancing down the hill.

"Go be crazy some place else."

She stopped, leaned against a tree. "Okay," she
said. "I guess that means you buy what they say about
him committing suicide."

There was a stick near Jim. He picked it up and
charged at her like a wild man. She jumped back and the
stick, punk to the core, snapped against the trunk of a
tree.

"You don't believe it, do you!" she said. "Hub Hawkins wouldn't kill himself. So why won't you help me?"

Jim gritted his teeth. He felt his blood surging. It
frightened him.

"If you know so much," he said hoarsely. "You tell
me."

She sat down on the hillside, just beyond his reach.
"Father prays for him a lot. I hear him. He has this
room with his own little altar in it. He goes there. He
doesn't know I'm listening. 'O, Lord,' he says. 'In thy
great mercy, guide the soul of Hub to your side.'"

"That's his *job*," Jim said, spluttering with anger.
"He's a *pastor*."

"True," she said. "But how come he's the *only* one

who seems to know for sure your dad is dead?"

"Shut up!"

Jim tried to leave. It was best not to argue. What he believed about his father's fate he had wrapped up tightly in a mourning bundle he carried around inside him. He knew what the outcome of the official inquiry had been — that his father had been mentally unsound, nuts. "It was his nerves," Jim's mother had tried to explain to him. "His nerves snapped on him." But that didn't explain him disappearing without a trace. They called it paranoid delusions, a persecution complex. They said it had been there for a long time. They said that he reached a point where he could no longer bear it.

Jim didn't believe a single word of it.

He tried to leave. He turned his back on Ruth Rose and started down the hill.

Which is when she blindsided him.

They rolled clear down the slope through drifts of dead leaves and they would have ended up in the creek if they hadn't smacked up against a rotting stump. It knocked the wind out of Jim, made his eyes roll around in their sockets. Then, before he could catch his breath, she rolled right on top of him, pinning his arms to the ground with her knees.

She growled in his face.

"Nobody listens to me," she said. "Nobody believes me."

He didn't move, not sure she wouldn't bite him, she was that close, that ferocious. Then she rolled off him, brushing the flaky leaves off her sweater and pulling them from the tangle of her hair.

"I've got proof," she said.

"Where?"

She tapped her skull. "Right here."

Jim lay with his arms akimbo, his knees up, working out the pain in his side. He turned his head. She was sullen, brooding.

He propped himself up on his elbows. He spoke very quietly. "You ever thought people might listen to you if you didn't knock them over?"

It was hard to tell in the gloom, but he thought he saw a smile flicker across her face. It gave him courage.

"Why don't you go to the cops?" he asked.

"Ha! With what I know about the cops?"

"Oh, right," he said and lay back quietly on the ground. But she didn't look like she was going to jump him again. So he edged himself up.

"Where do you think you're going?" she demanded.

"Didn't I tell you? I have a life," he said.

She parted the curtains of her bangs with her white fingers. "That's more than your daddy's got."

For a split second, he was too stunned to react. Then the tears came. They surprised him as much as they surprised her. He thought he had cried them all months ago. But he had only been damming them up, it seemed, for now they flowed out of him and dripped from his face onto the hillside. He made no attempt to stop them or mop them up. He sank back down to the ground and cried and his tears fell on the earth where they would eventually find their watery way through the loam to Incognito Creek.

"They were friends," she said. She didn't look at Jim. It was as if she were talking to herself. "Your daddy and Eldon, except he was Fish in those days. When they were kids. There's others — someone named Tuffy, someone else named Laverne. He talks to himself — Father, I mean. Well, it starts off like praying and then he drifts off and sometimes he sort of ends up a kid again. Like he's way gone. There's someone called Tabor, too. He says, 'Tabor will look after him,' or 'O, God, vouchsafe that Tabor can keep our secret.' He uses words like that — Bible words."

She looked at Jim expectantly. He wasn't crying anymore. He was watching her closely, wondering if the things she was saying were from a dream or if she was just pulling them out of thin air.

"All I want," she said, "is for you to find out who these people are. Something happened. A long time ago. I need to know what."

Jim didn't say anything. He was all talked out.

"Oh, yeah, and try to find out about a secret club or clubhouse," she added. "Can you do that? It's important." It was like she was a classmate asking him what their homework assignment was.

"I'll see," he muttered finally.

"We've got to put him behind bars," she said, "or else…" She looked at Jim eagerly. "Don't you want to know or else what?"

He shook his head.

"Or else he'll kill me," she explained.

"Oh," said Jim.

Ruth Rose looked at him peevishly. Then she looked curious. "You knew that about your daddy and Fisher, didn't you? Them growing up together?"

Jim didn't answer. He wasn't sure. As close as he had been to his father, he couldn't remember him talking much about his childhood — not about friends, anyway. He had talked about the farm and his folks and school — stuff like that. Jim, if he had ever thought about it at all, had just assumed that his father had been like him — alone a lot, satisfied to be that way for the most part.

As long as he could remember, Father Fisher had been around. At church, obviously, but at home, too. He had been a regular visitor. But Jim had never thought of him as a family friend. Friends stayed for supper or an evening of cards now and then. Father Fisher was never that kind of a visitor. He had never sat with Hub on the deck drinking a beer. But then he was a pastor. Hub used to go for walks with him. Towards the end, when Hub's nerves were going on him, he had seen a lot of the pastor.

Had they grown up together? Wouldn't Jim know something like that?

"Can you do it?" said Ruth Rose.

He looked at her like a zombie.

"Do what?"

"Find out," she said. "About...you know, Tuffy, Tabor, Laverne — anything."

It was no use arguing with her.

"Whatever you say," he replied. If he sounded less than convincing, she didn't try to stop him from leaving.

"I'm sorry for hurting you," she said. "And about...you know...It."

"What?" he said. He had jumped over to the other side of Incognito Creek. It wasn't much but it put something between them. When he turned, she seemed almost invisible, as if she had gathered up dusk all around her like a cape. As if she was just a part of the forest, a part of the coming night.

"About you losing your father," she said. "I know what it's like."

He looked at her. "No, you don't. You know what it's like losing *your* father."

He didn't turn around again when she called after him.

"It's worse for me," she shouted. "I've got a new one who wants to kill me."

The wind picked up just as Jim opened the gate from the cornfield. He had to fight to rope the gate closed again. The rope was fraying badly; he'd need to replace it. There was so much to do.

He stopped in his tracks. He had left the shovel at the dam. He stamped his foot like a three-year-old. He swore.

"You don't leave a tool out in the rain, Jimbo, unless you never plan on using it again."

He turned to go and retrieve it. But he couldn't. For all he knew, Ruth Rose was still out there prowling around, her teeth bared, worse than any wild dog with wildly impossible things pouring out of her black lips. She was a witch.

He heard the screen of the kitchen door slam back hard against the house, caught by the wind. He could just make out the form of his mother outlined in the doorway, the warm light of the kitchen behind her spilling out into the cool. Then she stepped out of his line of vision; the shrubbery and garden shed came between them.

Jim headed through the apple orchard until he caught a glimpse of her again. She was standing on the porch, talking to someone. A man. He was standing beyond the light of the doorway. Jim hurried, uneasy.

Out from behind the protective ranks of corn, the wind made him shiver, made him pull his open jacket closed around him. The zipper was broken. He hadn't even bothered showing it to his mom. When was she going to find time to fix it?

He got close enough that he could hear snatches of conversation from the porch. His mom was laughing. Now she was shaking the man's hand. Now the man stepped back up the steps to give her a hug. Big dark arms closed around her. She hugged him back.

Jim was at the garden shed now. He leaned against it, out of sight, watching.

It was okay. The man was going. His mother was already heading back inside.

Jim waited. The man was heading towards the front yard where his van was sitting, gleamy black under the yard light. Jim looked that way for the first time.

He knew the van, knew the scripture that was quoted in white scrolled letters on the side panels. The only thing he could read from where he was standing was what was written on the plastic wind foil across the front of the hood. "I Am The Lord Thy Saviour."

It was the car people around town called the Godmobile. Father Fisher's car.

4

His mom saw him before she shut the door. She waited to herd him inside with a warm hug. There were tears in her eyes.

"What did he want?" Jim asked.

His mother was mopping up a tear with the corner of her apron, but there was a smile on her face.

"He was looking for his daughter," she said as she cleared the kitchen table of tea things.

Jim hung up his coat, kicked off his boots, stopped himself from blurting out anything.

"Apparently she roams. Lettie Kitchen — you know Lettie down on the Glenshee Road, the one who makes the horrible green Jello with miniature marshmallows for every church social — she phoned Father to let him know she'd seen the girl on the tracks heading up this way."

Snoot was curled up on the rocker by the woodstove. Jim picked her up and held her against his face. She was full of woodstove warmth. Jim took the seat and rocked a bit. It was strange to hear his mother so chatty. Obviously, Father Fisher's visit hadn't just been about Ruth Rose.

She was filling the soup tureen. Jim should have been helping but the stove and the kitten held him captive.

"The girl's quite a problem for them, I gather. Poor Nancy."

Nancy was Mrs. Fisher. Ruth Rose's mother. She was the kind of person you said "poor Nancy" about. She was in a wheelchair, but that wasn't the reason. She had lost an unborn child in the car crash that had crippled her and killed her husband. But that wasn't the reason, either. She seemed helpless in some other way, almost haunted. She was sweet, though. Everybody at the Church of the Blessed Transfiguration liked her a lot, remarked about what a saintly soul she was.

Iris Hawkins carried the tureen to the table. She glanced at Jim and smiled to see him with the kitten on his lap. Then she returned to the counter for bread and butter. Reluctantly, Jim got up and washed his hands at the kitchen sink.

They sat down. Holding his hand, bowing her head and closing her eyes, his mother said grace. Jim didn't bow his head or close his eyes. As far as he was concerned, there was no God to thank for anything.

Jim had filled the sky with prayers — stood out in the middle of the field on clear days so that no roof, no trees, no clouds could stop his prayers from reaching the ear of the Maker. He had promised the Almighty elaborate penance, a life dedicated to helping the poor — whatever God ordained. But God had done nothing.

So now, Jim sat in respectful silence. The respect was for his mother.

His mother ladled rich corn and potato chowder into his bowl. He cut thick slices of bread, poured them each a glass of water. There was still a smile playing around the edge of his mother's face. She caught him looking at her and grinned.

"What's up?" he asked, taking a bowl of soup.

She took a deep, wobbly breath. "The church..." she said, then stopped to compose herself. "The church has decided — well, almost, anyway — to assume our mortgage."

"What does that mean?"

"It means that if everything goes according to plan, they're going to pay the bank the money we had to borrow this year, and we'll pay back the church at a lower interest rate and with much better terms. Take as long as we want, was the way Father put it." Her voice was breaking with emotion.

When Jim didn't reply, his mother added, "It's a real blessing, Jim."

He nodded and ate some soup. He knew they had money problems. It was the reason his mother had taken the job at the soap factory. He wondered if this meant she could stop now. He didn't ask, didn't want to seem too eager about it in case she thought her working bothered him.

"So he didn't just come out looking for his daughter?" he said.

"Oh, he was looking for her, all right. He had wanted to tell us about the mortgage business but he hadn't wanted to mention it until it was in the bag."

"And it's in the bag?"

"Pretty much," said his mother, crossing her fingers. "We're lucky, Jim, to have such a caring community." She paused with a spoonful of soup halfway to her mouth as if she were going to say something else. Something about him going to church. But she changed her mind.

Jim kept his thoughts to himself. They ate in silence for a moment. There was just the sound of spoon against bowl, the clicking that came from the wood-stove when it was cranking out the heat, and occasionally the sound of the wind blustering outside, shaking the trees, whipping around the tarp that covered the firewood.

"He grew up with Dad, didn't he?" Jim tried to make his voice sound casual, just table talk.

"Father Fisher? Yes." She looked at him quizzically, as if surprised that he didn't know. "Father's a few years older, but they were pals, I guess. You know the big old brownstone place up the hill this side of the McCoys? That was the house he grew up in. His father Wilfred Fisher was the richest man on the Twelfth Line. The richest man in this corner of the township."

Jim nodded. He knew the house. It was boarded up like a lot of places on the line. But it was much more imposing, set on a hill with a long circular drive. There was even a stone wall along the road and the remains of a wrought-iron fence. People around these parts didn't go in for such showiness — didn't have the money for it.

"How come Father Fisher doesn't live there?" Jim asked.

"Probably couldn't afford to on a minister's salary. Anyway, what would Nancy do in a cavernous place like that? They'd need ramps and...Lord, can you imagine the heating bill..."

Jim was only half listening. He was busy trying to imagine Father Fisher as his father's pal.

His mother started talking about farm stuff — some problems they were having with the milk separator, how she thought maybe one of her hens was going broody, how someone might phone tonight about seeing the Malibu and what to say if they did. "I was going to sell it as is, but Orm McCoy convinced me that with a little body work, we could get a really good price on it. An antique. Imagine."

Jim listened up, put aside his resentment about selling his father's car, put aside the incident in the woods.

At first he had hated it when his mother started talking to him about grown-up things. There was always stuff breaking down, needing parts, needing attention. When his father had been alive this had been exactly the kind of thing his folks had jawed over at the supper table, and it had been fine as background noise while he thought his own thoughts. Now he had to pay attention. His mother had never said it in so many words, but she expected him to figure out what jobs he was supposed to do.

"How do you expect me to fill his shoes?" he wanted to say. But he kept it to himself.

His mother cleaned up while he sat at the kitchen table and did some homework. But it was hard to concentrate. He kept getting flashes of Ruth Rose's face hovering over him, ready to bite his nose off.

"There were other kids, too, weren't there?" he said, out of the blue, trying to sound conversational.

"What's that?"

"Other friends. Dad and Father Fisher and some others?"

His question met with a stony silence. Then the sound of water and a scrub brush working hard.

"I'm surprised your father would have told you about that." She didn't sound especially suspicious or alarmed. Just surprised. Jim dared to go on.

"Why?"

He listened while his mother rinsed the soup pot and put it in the drying rack. "Well, it was something he didn't much like to talk about, that's all."

Jim swivelled around in his chair. "What happened?"

His mother glanced at him over her shoulder. She was frowning a bit, and part of him wanted to say forget it, but he couldn't make himself.

"Francis," she said. "That was his name." Jim's interest deflated a little — Francis wasn't one of the names Ruth Rose had mentioned — but he nodded for his mother to go on.

"Well, it was long before I arrived on the scene," she said, "when Hub was young. Francis died. A terrible death. Hub was around seventeen, I guess. It hit him pretty hard. He was in the eleventh grade, never did finish his year."

Iris Hawkins went back to washing. Jim didn't want to push her too far but, as it turned out, she was only collecting her thoughts.

"Died on New Year's Eve. In a fire — a fire he started himself."

"You mean it was suicide?"

His mother shrugged. "At the inquest they called it death by misadventure. At least, I think that's what it was called. I didn't know him. I didn't even know your father then but he talked about it from time to time. It troubled him."

"Does death by misadventure mean it was a mistake, kind of? Like he was playing with matches and it got out of hand?"

Iris nodded and went back to her work. Then she dried her hands and turned to face him. "Since you're so morbidly interested, the boy was a known arsonist. A pyromaniac. Do you know what that is?"

Jim nodded hesitantly. "Someone who likes fire?"

"Someone who *starts* fires," his mother said. "I like fires, in their place. This Frankie kid, he started all sorts of them in the area. Some of the old-timers could tell you. At first, I guess, it was just mischief, an outhouse or a tumbledown shed. But it got worse. He burned down a chicken shack up at Lar Perkins' father's place and killed twenty layers and fifty meat birds. Then he hit a small barn at Jock Boomhower's with a couple of cows in it. That's when he got caught. Sent off to jail."

"But he came back?" asked Jim.

"Came back and burned down the house his family had lived in. Can you imagine? Of course, no one was living in it then. His family had moved. Wilf Fisher had bought the property and was using the old place to store hay."

"In a house?"

"It was a very old house. A log cabin. You know the place. It's in the low field just east of the cut road, below the Fisher mansion."

Jim knew the field, all right, but he couldn't remember any house.

"It's just a rubble heap now," said his mother. "Mostly grown over. Heavens, it must be twenty-five years ago, at least." He saw her do the math in her head. "1972. New Year's Eve, 1972."

His mother's eyes glanced up at the clock above the kitchen table and Jim took the hint. He turned back to his homework, but his mind was buzzing. A moment later, his mother scruffled his hair as she passed him on her way upstairs.

"I'm going to take a shower," she said. But she turned at the parlour door. "I remember now. The family was called Tufts. Francis Tufts."

As soon as she was gone, Jim sat back in his chair thinking through what he had learned. Did Ruth Rose, who knew everything, know about this fire? And Francis Tufts — it wasn't much of a stretch from that to Tuffy. But what did it have to do with her stepfather or his own father's disappearance?

Nothing. It was ancient history. And he would probably end up as cracked as she was if he started thinking that way.

Snoot suddenly jumped onto his lap and Jim cried out in astonishment, which frightened the kitten who jumped right off, taking some flesh from his leg with her. Her sharp little claws had gone right through his jeans. He rubbed his thigh and settled back to work.

His mother kissed him goodbye on the way out, went over for the hundredth time the business about locking the doors and checking the woodstove and which lights to leave on.

"I know, I know," he said, submitting to a second and third bone-crushing hug.

"Hot cinnamon rolls for breakfast?" she asked. Jim looked appropriately blissful. The Sunflower Bakery was just firing up when she got off work, and sometimes she would stop by on her way home. She came home stinking like soap. "I'm going to have to rub myself down with a fish," she had said once. But, no matter how tired she was, she would walk out to the road with him every morning and wait for the school bus.

Jim watched her drive off in the truck, locking up as soon as she was gone. Then he went into the sitting room.

The family photos lay loose in an old, carved wooden box with a hinged lid. It was called a monk's bench and the carvings on the front were kind of churchy with monks praying. His mother wasn't sure if it had ever really belonged to a monk, but it was supposed to be where one would keep his stuff. Now it was filled with photos and the odd Christmas card, yellowing newspaper clippings.

After a few minutes, Jim stopped rifling through the stuff in a random kind of way and took out a huge armful. Sitting cross-legged on the rag carpet, he started a more thorough search.

Here were his father and mother when they were young, dressed up for some formal, standing beside the Malibu. Here was Jim with Hub at the curling club's annual father-and-son bonspiel. Here was his father pretending to saw Jim's bike in half with a chainsaw. Jim laughed.

He got out a second and a third armful, sorting the older pictures into a separate pile and then studying them carefully.

Finally, he hit pay dirt. A black-and-white snapshot of three boys in T-shirts sitting on the front stoop of an old log cabin squinting into the light. On the back someone had written: "The Three Musketeers." And under it: "Frankie, 'Fish' and little Hub."

Little Hub Hawkins was in shorts. His bare feet didn't even reach the ground. He looked about twelve. Fish was a teenager, a senior by the size of him. He was leaning against the stoop with his chest puffed out and his arms crossed like Mr. Clean. Frankie was pointing at him and laughing. Frankie was older than Hub and younger than Fish and kind of gawky looking. His hair looked white in the photo — the colour of sunlight on a window. Fish's hair was black, longish with wide sideburns, like pictures Jim had seen from the sixties. Father Fisher's hair was the same colour now, though not so long.

That was when the phone rang.

Jim nearly jumped out of his skin. He got up awkwardly, his legs filled with pins and needles. He hobbled into the kitchen to the wall phone above the table. Glancing at the clock, he saw that it was almost midnight.

Who would be phoning so late? The phone rang again, too loud in the silent house.

Dad.

The thought made his knees buckle.

He's phoning to tell us where he is, why he left so suddenly, why he didn't even say goodbye.

On the eleventh ring, it suddenly occurred to Jim that it might be the factory to say his mother had been injured. That broke the spell. He snapped up the phone and spoke into the receiver breathlessly, as if he had run a mile.

"Hello?"

The voice at the other end of the phone whispered, "Did you talk to him? Did you tell him anything?"

Jim didn't speak. He guessed who it was, but he was too stunned to say a word.

"What's the matter? Is there someone there?"

Jim didn't answer.

"Say 'you've got the wrong number' if there's somebody there and I'll get back to you some other time."

Jim swallowed and took a deep breath. "You're scaring me," he said, sounding like a six-year-old.

Now it was her turn to go silent, and in the silence Jim heard a man's voice. The voice said, "Ruth Rose?" Then there was nothing but a sharp click and a dial tone.

5

Jim was tired all the next day but after school he dropped off his backpack at home, changed into his grubby clothes and set off for the beaver dam, bent on recovering the shovel he had left behind and undoing whatever the beavers might have gotten up to overnight.

Ruth Rose beat him to it. He could hear her singing to herself good and loud.

There was nothing to stop him from heading back home. But as he stood listening he realized she was straining at something as she sang. So he made his way soundlessly through the sopping wet grass until he caught sight of her.

She was hacking away at the dam, the same cavity he had worked at the day before. But she wasn't using his shovel. It was leaning against a tree along with Gladys. She was using a pickaxe, and she wasn't squeamish about it, either.

She swung it high above her head and brought it down into the guck up to its hilt. She had muscle, all right. She hauled at the axe and brought up a great gob of putrefied vegetation. The water spilled into the crevice and on through the busted dam but not with much force. By now, it was good and low.

She stopped singing. Without looking back, she

said in a good clear voice, "You might as well come out. You're not going to catch me giving Gladys a soaker."

Jim blushed. He stood up tall, stepped out into the open and made his way towards her. Her red T-shirt was stained with sweat and splatters of mud. He looked out across the flats where the water had been so high just the day before.

"You did a good job," he managed to say.

She scrinched up her nose, rubbed it, looking a little flustered, as if she wasn't used to compliments. "The beavers didn't do any building last night, as far as I could tell. I guess Gladys deserves some of the credit."

Jim laughed nervously.

Ruth Rose came down off the dam and made her way towards him with her pickaxe over her shoulder like one of the seven dwarfs, but which one? Grumpy? Dopey? Crazy?

"Did you carry that all the way from town?" he asked.

"No," she said. "There was a work crew on the tracks. They gave me a lift." He wondered, from the hesitant way she said it, whether maybe she had stolen the pickaxe.

She put it down and went to get Gladys, planting her in the spot at the mouth of the breach where Jim had placed her the day before. She made Gladys wave to him. Jim gulped. Waved back.

"Care to give her another dousing?" Ruth Rose said. "I won't peek this time, promise."

Jim turned red.

"It's your call," she said.

There was something altogether different about

her manner today. She joined him again and they walked up the lane a bit, found a dry log and sat down.

"I'm on my medication," she said, as if she had been reading his mind. "Bummer, eh? Just when it looks like I'm a human being after all, it turns out I'm a real nut-case who has to be drugged."

He looked at her and there was a glassy look in her eyes.

She looked down, picked up a small branch, broke it twig by twig.

"This isn't the real me," she said. "But the thing is, the fiend you met yesterday wasn't the real me, either. I'm a mess, okay? I hate the drugs, but if I don't take them like a good girl…"

She didn't finish the sentence.

"I didn't talk to Father yesterday," said Jim. "Honest." He told her about the pastor being at the house when he got back. "Did you get in trouble?"

She smiled a kind of loopy smile. "I'm always in trouble."

Jim looked sideways at her. "Does he hit you?"

Then she really laughed. "It's much worse than that. You know what he does when I'm being *recalcitrant,* as he puts it?" Ruth Rose leaned up close. "He prays for me."

She seemed to enjoy the surprise on his face. "He just drops to his knees, right there — wherever it is — and folds his hands in front of his face and he starts in praying for my *recalcitrant* soul. That's what he did last night. Once he did it in the middle of a supermart. In the canned vegetable aisle."

Jim shook his head in astonishment. "That must be awful."

She nodded and was silent. "He prays all the time." Then she smirked. "Like a hawk."

The sky was plugged up with clouds, the temperature was dropping. Jim noticed that now that she wasn't working anymore, Ruth Rose was shivering, her narrow shoulders up high, her shoulder blades sticking out like wings.

"I'll get your jacket," he said.

Her black leather jacket was hanging from a poplar bough. Something on the lapel glittered with reflected light. A mirror the size of a campaign button. She had been watching for him.

He looked at himself in the mirror. The pimple on his nose said he was fourteen. The bewilderment in his eyes said he was going on four.

"Don't you go to school?" he asked, when he got back.

She shook her head. "I'm home-schooled."

Poor Nancy, thought Jim.

"Before the accident, Mom taught public school. We work all morning and then I have the afternoon off. I'm not stupid, you know."

"Didn't say you were," said Jim.

"I know you didn't," she said. "But you were thinking it. You were thinking what kind of dumb chick spends her spare time snooping around trying to prove her stepfather is a murderer."

Jim looked at her. "Actually, I was thinking what kind of a maniac goes around doing that."

She smiled in a maniac kind of way. Then she thrust her hands into her jacket pockets and dug out two slightly battered Hershey bars. She offered one to Jim.

"I owe you this for yesterday," she said. "I didn't know how to talk to you."

"That," said Jim, taking the candy, "is the biggest understatement of the year."

"It's just that there didn't seem an easy way to start. You know, it's a pretty tough thing to try to tell someone. So I kind of used the Ruth Rose Way."

"You mean roll over somebody like a freight train?"

"Not exactly," she said. "I was thinking more of the track than the train. The Ruth Rose Way goes straight to where it's going, cuts through people's yards instead of going around, cuts across roads wherever it wants. Cars stop. People stay clear."

Jim wasn't sure what to say. "Well, thanks for helping with the dam."

She bit off a mouthful of chocolate. "Hey, I'm asking you for help so I figure I should return the favour."

The chocolate in Jim's mouth tasted unpalatable all of a sudden. He had been enjoying sitting on a log sharing some candy with her, like ordinary kids. But nothing about Ruth Rose was ordinary.

"Did you find out anything?" she asked.

Jim swallowed and wrapped up the rest of the bar. He started to hand it back to her but a flicker in her eyes stopped him.

Everything was quiet for a moment. Then he told her about the photograph of the Three Musketeers, about Frankie, the boy with the white hair. Francis Tufts.

Her eyes lit up. "Tuffy!" she said. Jim shrugged, but he was proud of himself nonetheless.

"Could be," he said. Then he told her about Francis dying in the log house on New Year's Eve of 1972.

"Holy cow," she said. He watched her try to incorporate his news into her plot.

"I didn't find out anything about the others," he said.

"That's okay," she said. "You will. I know it."

Jim took no pleasure from her encouragement. "It's all ancient history. I don't know how it's supposed to help."

"I don't know how, either," she replied. "But I know why. Because a life might depend on it. *Mine*."

Jim looked away. He wanted out and yet there was something holding him captive.

"You really think he'd do anything to you?"

She looked at him with surprise. "Unless I do something first," she said. "He's known for awhile that I was on to him. Now he acts as if maybe I'm getting too close for comfort."

Jim fought off a minor panic attack. "Don't get mad," he said as calmly as he could. "But why do you hate him? Because he prays for you?"

"I don't know if I can explain it," she said. "I hated him from the start. Hated him for marrying my mother. The doctors tell me that's pretty natural. A lot of kids hate their steps, at first. But it's more than that."

She paused, staring off across the wet lowlands to the meadow beyond, where a wind they could not feel down in the hollow was bending the heads of the tall grass.

"When he prays, he always starts out by saying how he himself is a sinner, a great sinner. I know, I know, we're *all* sinners. That's how the Church of the Blessed Transfiguration stays in business. But when Father Fisher says it, man, he sounds like he *means* it. I can feel it in here." She pounded her fist against her breast bone. "Which is why I started watching him. Eavesdropping. Which is why I know what happened."

She glanced nervously at Jim, afraid he was going to run away on her.

But Jim stood his ground. "There was this bully at school," he said. "I hated him. He beat me up a couple of times. I hated everything he did. If he was eating a candy bar, I thought, what a greedy pig. If he scored a touchdown, I thought, what a show-off. One day I saw him helping an old lady across a street and I thought, he's probably going to steal her purse."

"Did he?"

"No," said Jim. "That's the point. He wasn't so bad, except for being a pain in the butt. It was only because I hated him I figured everything he did was bad."

Ruth Rose frowned, looked down again so that her hair hid her face. She folded up her chocolate bar and put it in her pocket. Then she got up and, without a backward glance at Jim, left.

It took Jim a moment to recover. "Hey," he yelled. "What did I say?"

She stopped, but she didn't turn around. "Forget it."

"Ruth Rose," he shouted, surprised at how snappish it sounded, as if he was yelling at Snoot to get off the table.

Then she turned around. "Listen, if you can't take this seriously —"

"I do," Jim interrupted.

"We're not talking here about a schoolyard bully."

"I was just —"

"You were just telling me a story," she said. "Like this is the Brady Bunch or something."

"Okay, I'm sorry," said Jim. "I want to know what happened."

She came closer, stared at him and, despite the medication, it seemed to Jim as if she were looking right inside him.

"No, you don't," she said. "You're too afraid."

Then she started to walk away again, towards the woods.

He couldn't let her go just like that. Letting go was a problem he had.

"I am not afraid!" he shouted.

"You aren't ready," she shouted back.

"Ready for what?"

"You don't want to face the fact that your daddy is dead. D-E-A-D."

Jim felt like he was teetering, suddenly. On the edge of a rushing stream and not sure whether to jump or go looking for a bridge. Not sure he could clear it, not sure he wouldn't drown if he fell in. Ruth Rose was on the other side of that stream and she wasn't the kind of guide he would have wished to lead him anywhere. But what was there anymore on this side of the stream?

He took a deep breath, let it out slowly. Leapt.

"Tell me," he said. "Please."

She turned and walked back towards him. When she was close enough, she looked him in the eye long and hard. He didn't flinch.

"Your dad saw Father a bunch of times right before he disappeared."

"I know," said Jim. "On account of his nerves. Father came out to the farm. They went on these long walks."

"And your dad came to our house, too. Father didn't like him coming over. He always took him to the church where they could talk in private. The last time was September twenty-fifth."

The twenty-fifth was the day before Jim's father went missing. He nodded for her to go on.

"They had a big argument. Something about a letter and what they were going to do about it. It wasn't the first letter, either, but it was the worst, as far as I could tell. Your dad was real upset. Father kept trying to cool him down."

"I thought you said they met at the church?"

"They did," said Ruth Rose. "I followed them there. There was no one around so they could talk more freely without Father having to shush your dad up all the time."

"So what did they say?" demanded Jim.

"I told you. They were talking about this letter. Your dad mentioned Tuffy. Father told him not to talk about Tuffy. Not ever."

She paused. "I couldn't hear much. The sacristy door is solid oak. I heard bits and pieces of stuff. 'She's got nothing to go on,' Father said more than once. I think they were talking about someone called Laverne. I heard your dad saying, 'I've suffered long enough.' Then I heard Father say this: 'Tomorrow's a good day.' Those were his exact words. 'Tomorrow's a good day.'"

Jim swallowed hard.

"And the thing is," said Ruth Rose, "the next day Father wasn't around. He wasn't at the church. I checked. And where was your mother, Jim? *She* was at the church, decorating it with the altar guild for the Harvest Festival. You think Father didn't know she was going to be away from the farm all day?"

Jim's chin twitched. "Why didn't you say something then?" he asked. "I mean at the inquest."

"Me?" she said. "Who'd believe me? Anyway, I didn't have any proof. So I decided to get some. I figured the letters had to be blackmail. I figured, since I couldn't find them around our place, they were probably hidden in the sacristy somewhere. So one night, I broke in."

Jim stared at her incredulously. "Into the church?"

Ruth Rose nodded proudly, but her expression soured. "I got in okay but then the fuzz came."

"The cops?"

She nodded. "I got arrested," she said. "Father called them. Can you believe it? His own *daughter*."

"So you told the police what you were doing," he said with a kind of weary resignation, already imagining the scene.

"You bet I did," she said. "I told them about Father murdering your dad and that the proof was probably in the church office somewhere."

"Let me guess," he said. "They didn't go for it."

She looked at him with something approaching a wicked grin lighting up her pale face. "I kinda pulled a Ruth Rose Way on them, I guess. Went ballistic. Gave one of them a black eye," she added. "They released me into Father's custody. He didn't press charges but he made sure I wasn't around for the inquest."

"What do you mean?"

Ruth Rose's grin dissolved. "I was packed off somewhere. I don't want to talk about it."

Jim didn't want to talk about it, either. There was something more pressing he needed to know if he was to believe anything she said.

"So now I know why you couldn't get anybody to listen to you back then. But why are you trying now? And why me?"

Ruth Rose suddenly looked tired. She sniffed, rubbed her nose.

"I need your help," she said. "Yeah, don't say it — I need lots of help. But seriously, I'm afraid. Father's really weird. Weird like...well, almost like your father was last fall."

"What are you saying?"

She looked him straight in the eye. "I think you know what I'm saying."

Jim could feel the anger rising in him. He tried to remember that he was talking to a crazy person. She didn't know anything. For all he knew, she was making it all up.

"You're saying, this blackmailer was blackmailing both of them — Father Fisher and my father. Then it stopped...after my dad disappeared. But now it's started again."

She didn't move a muscle.

"Listen," he said, his voice belligerent. "Maybe my father knew something — something Fisher did. Maybe. And maybe that's what drove him nuts, 'cause he wanted to tell but he didn't want to get Fisher in trouble. But don't try and tell me he did anything wrong. You didn't know him. He was the best. And no freak is going to tell me different."

She didn't punch him or argue, but he could see she was hurt. Well, she deserved it. She was nothing but trouble.

She looked down, looked up again with a little scornful smile. "Like I said. You're not ready for this."

He was going to shout at her. But he didn't want to shout. Didn't want to be dragged into her game.

"All I meant," she said, "was that things cooled down after Hub disappeared. Father was gloomy for a while but he wasn't on edge."

"Yeah, well, you'd be gloomy if you lost a friend,"

said Jim. "If you had any." He swallowed hard. He hadn't meant to say that.

For once, Ruth Rose was quiet. Then, after a long silence, she looked past Jim up the lane. "You ever wonder what happened that day at the cedar grove?" she asked, her voice pitched almost too low to hear.

Jim's head snapped up. "Are you kidding? I never thought about anything else for most of the year."

"Well, try this," she said. There was a look in her eyes as if what she was going to say was some kind of test. "Your dad meets up with Father that day, just like he told him to the night before at the church. He's somebody your dad trusts, right? They go out for one of their long walks or for a drive, maybe, to talk things over some more. There's a million places up this way they could go and nobody'd see them. Half the farms on this road are deserted. The wilderness stretches halfway to Hudson Bay. They could have gone anywhere."

Reluctantly Jim nodded, feeling a little sick.

"Your dad wants to do something, talk to somebody, basically cave in — that's what it sounded like to me the night before. Father doesn't want him to. Father says it's going to be all right. But it isn't going to be all right if your dad starts blabbing."

"Blabbing about *what*?"

"If I knew that, I wouldn't be here," she said. "Maybe what happened to Tuffy."

"That was an accident," snapped Jim. "Death by misadventure."

Ruth Rose raised her eyebrows. The gesture infuriated Jim. Nothing was an accident to her, he thought.

"Okay, okay," she said. "Something else. That's

what we've got to find out. But something they were in together." Jim was about to object when her eyes lit up. "You just don't get it, do you? You won't believe your daddy could do anything wrong. Fine, don't. But let me finish."

"Okay," said Jim. "So finish."

She stared at him slack-jawed, shaking her head as if she had given up on him entirely. To his surprise, he didn't want her to give up.

"Go on," he said quietly.

She sighed. "They go somewhere where no one's around. Fisher does him in. Maybe it wasn't intentional. Maybe they were having this fight and he killed him by mistake. But it's done. So then he drives the car down here and leaves it so it looks like your dad just abandoned it."

"How?" said Jim. "There were just my dad's footprints down here. Nobody else had been in the car. They had those forensic guys go over it. They don't miss stuff like that. There were no 'alien fibres' — that's the way they put it. Nothing."

"I'm not talking about aliens," shouted Ruth Rose.

Jim couldn't talk anymore. His head was clogged up with painful images. It wasn't as if he hadn't thought them before — thought of his father meeting up with some horrible end. He had imagined biker gangs and bears. Murderers of every shape and size had paraded through his nightmares. But he had never put a real face on the killer.

Ruth Rose lightly touched his shoulder. "Hey, I'm outa here," she said. Her anger seemed to have passed. "You listened to me, at least. That's more than anyone else ever did. Thanks. If you find out anything, you could...you know..."

She left, headed back towards Ruth Rose Way. She left her pickaxe behind. Jim was going to call after her, when he looked more closely at the tool and realized that it wasn't hers, after all, and she hadn't stolen it from any railroad crew, either.

She had lied. There were initials carved into the butt end. HH. It was his father's pickaxe.

6

ector Menzies had been a newspaper boy at the *Ladybank Expositor* when his mother was a reporter. He had been a cub reporter himself when his mother took over the reins as editor. And he had become editor when she took over from her father, Salvator Menzies, as publisher. Hector was publisher now and he was a busy man. But not so busy he couldn't spare a few minutes for Jim Hawkins.

Jim went to the *Expositor* office the next day after school. He hadn't thought to phone and make an appointment but, luckily, Hec passed by the front office just as Dorothy was explaining to Jim that he would have to come by some other time.

Hec led Jim into his cubby-hole of an office. It wasn't much for the publisher of a newspaper — a ceiling you could touch if you cared to reach up, no window, no carpet and an elephantine desk that just about filled the space and looked old enough to have been Noah's desk on the Ark.

"We don't have any money for frills," Hec said to Jim. "The circulation of the *Expositor* has grown in direct proportion to the population of Ladybank over the last hundred years, which is to say, not at all."

When Hub Hawkins had disappeared, there had been lots of regional press coverage of the story, even in Ottawa and Kingston. Not because Jim's father was famous, or anything, but because it was a mystery. Besides, Hub had been a pillar of the community: a deputy reeve of North Blandford Township, a hardworking board member of the Ladybank and District Public Library, and a pretty good skip at the local curling club, which had once sent a team to the Eastern Ontario finals in Cornwall.

Hector Menzies, although old enough to be Hub's father, had been second on that team and a friend of the Hawkins family ever since. His grandfatherly friendship had come in handy during the awful weeks of the previous fall when the farm had been under siege. Not from grasshoppers or groundhogs — things a farmer learns to cope with — but from news men and women banging on the door at any time of the day or night. They parked their cars and satellite-rigged vans all over the place — in the way of the barn so that Iris couldn't get her cattle out to pasture, in the way of the fields so that good neighbours couldn't get in to help with the harvest. It was hard enough for Jim and Iris, but the media hounds made it even worse.

Until Hector stepped in.

Hector Protector.

Hec set himself up as a kind of self-appointed spokesman for the family, deflecting the advances of the most obnoxious snoops and bringing some order into an otherwise chaotic situation.

He never once used his privileged insider status to benefit his own insignificant little weekly. No glimpses of the family in mourning, no scoops. He kept private what he felt deserved to remain private. Which was pretty well everything.

Jim had put Hec out of his mind once the siege was

over, but he was glad to see him again, despite the memories his lined old face evoked. He squeezed into the only other chair in Hec's office. The computer terminal looked out of place on the desk, and Hec looked out of place sitting behind it.

"What can I do for you, Jimbo?" he said.

"I want to find out about a fire that happened up near us in 1972."

Hec's forehead wrinkled for a moment. He looked like he was going through a file in his head that included so many fires and car crashes and hunting accidents no reasonable human could hope to keep track of them.

"A kid died in it," Jim added hurriedly. "A kid named Francis Tufts. It was New Year's. Don't you have it on your computer or something?"

A light went on in Hector's grizzled face. He smiled, raising one of his bushy eyebrows. "Oh, I can find what you're looking for since you've got the date and all. But I'm still a newspaperman, Jimbo, and a newspaperman depends on a sharp memory even more than he depends on a sharp pencil." He patted the computer monitor. "You won't find it in here," he said. "What you want is hard copy."

He pushed himself up and out of his chair. "Follow me."

Jim followed him down a long corridor with offices on one side and a wide sloped counter all along the other. Under it, row and rows of shelves buckled with the weight of bound volumes of the *Expositor*. Hec dragged one off the shelf and laid it down on the counter at eye level: 1972 was embossed in gold on the cover.

"Voilà!" he said, opening the volume to the very

first page. "Easy as pie. The lead story in the first issue of the year."

There before Jim's eyes was a grey and grainy photograph of a log cabin kind of slumping in the middle, as if a giant had sat on it. The windows and door were boarded up, but the stoop was recognizable as the one where the Three Musketeers had been sitting in the photo at home. Above the picture was the headline: BOY DIES IN NEW YEAR'S EVE BLAZE.

Jim looked at Hec. If he was wondering what Jim wanted with the story, he didn't show it. He just seemed proud to be able to provide the information.

Jim saw that the article continued on the following page. "Can I photocopy this?" he asked.

Hec shook his head. "Newspaper isn't meant for the long haul. It's meant to get read and put in the bottom of your bird cage. See how fragile the paper is?"

Fragile and fading fast, thought Jim, suddenly worried that he might not even have time to read it.

"But," said Hec. "I can give you a pen with the *Expositor* logo on it and a sheet or two of yellow foolscap and you're free to copy it out longhand."

So Jim did. He copied the whole thing. He wrote in his best hand as if it were the good draft of a school assignment.

A New Year's Eve blaze took the life of former North Blandford resident, nineteen-year-old Francis Tufts. The fire burned to the ground a local landmark. The log cabin, situated on the Twelfth Line, and once lived in by the Tufts family, was in the news several years ago, when it was believed to be haunted.

The fire was reported by Jock Boomhower

who was attending a get-together across the road at the home of Purvis Poole. The volunteer fire brigade made good time considering the snowy conditions but was unable to save the building. Volunteer Fire Chief, August Sweeney, stated that they had no idea there was anyone inside. It was not until Ontario Provincial Police were combing the site the following morning that they discovered the charred remains of the Tufts boy. He was identified by a silver allergy bracelet. Contacting his parents now living in Brockville, the police were able to ascertain that the boy had been expected home for Christmas but had not shown up.

The house was being used by a neighbour, Wilfred Fisher, to store hay. An inquest will be held into the death, but according to Constable Lorne Braithewaite, there do not seem to be any signs of foul play. Among the remains around the boy were found several beer bottles and a 40 ounce rye bottle, all empty.

Heavy snowfall through the night obliterated any footsteps leading to the building so it was not clear from which direction the boy might have journeyed. Constable Braithewaite noted the next morning that even the tracks of the fire truck and the sizeable area the fire fighters had disturbed in their efforts were completely blanketed by the new snowfall.

Francis's presence back in the Ladybank area was a surprise. The house had been the last dwelling place of the deceased and his family before leaving the area five years ago.

Jim stopped to rest his fingers. He stared at the photograph, tried to imagine stepping inside a house that had once been your home, at night, with the windows boarded up, and finding it filled to the rafters with hay. It would be like a nightmare, he thought.

Francis had been serving a sentence in the Orillia Reformatory, sent there in 1967 after being convicted in juvenile court of several cases of arson in and around Ladybank. His arrest came about in a most unusual way. In 1967, during the week of August 8-15, the Tufts family had reported a number of strange occurrences. Laverne Tufts claimed that "Stove lids danced in the air, the teapots jumped off the stove into the wood box, three flat irons walked down the staircase and dishes pranced on the dining room table."

A neighbour, Ormond McCoy, declared that a bone thrown out of the home, time and time again, had always returned to the house for no explicable reason.

On the Sunday directly following the report of "Ghosts," a flotilla of cars and the chopper from Ottawa television station CJOH arrived at the Tufts home. "Ghost Hunters" and paranormal experts descended upon the community from as far away as Buffalo, New York.

Believing there had to be a more reasonable explanation for the occurrences, the Perth OPP detachment stationed an inspector on the property for the night. That inspector was Lorne Braithewaite, a rookie at the time, fresh out of Police College. He remembers having tea at the kitchen table with Mrs. Tufts at about 11:00 PM when 14-year-old Francis arrived home smelling strongly of gasoline. When Braithewaite received a call shortly thereafter regarding a fire at a farm down the road and later learned that arson was suspected, he returned to the Tufts household and apprehended Francis for questioning.

Not only did Francis plead guilty to setting the fire, but he also owned up to several other fires in the area. As well, he ended speculation by admitting that he had been the "ghost" of the Tufts home. The youth was sent away and his family moved from North Blandford. Francis is survived by his parents Wendall and Laverne Tufts and his younger brother Stanley, now residents of Brockville.

Jim's hand was shaking. He reread the last sentence, scarcely able to believe it. Laverne was Tuffy's mother. He reread the whole article and then stood leaning against the wooden counter, thinking.

The ghost incident had happened when Francis Tufts was fourteen. The white-haired Musketeer had looked around that age — around Jim's age — in the photo. So Eldon Fisher and Hub had been friends of the fire starter right around the time of the haunting of the Tufts house.

Jim closed the newspaper yearbook. He didn't want to think about the log cabin any longer, or the flames that had consumed the boy trapped inside.

His mother was in town to do her weekly grocery shopping and they had agreed to meet at the library. He had said he had some research to do and would be there at five. It was important that he not lie to her. It had not been all that long ago that he had been so twisted up inside he couldn't speak, so twisted up he had tried, more than once, to kill himself. Ruth Rose had been right about the tree jumping. Jim had lied to his mother a lot in that bleak time. He couldn't talk but he would write on the pad on the kitchen table that he had been playing in the woods or in the sand pits up the road at Purvis Poole's or over at Jesse Desjardin's.

He didn't want to have to lie to her ever again.

Billy Bones had brought him back to his senses. Jim thought about Billy now. He thought about Ruth Rose. Maybe crazy people were the only ones he could associate with anymore. Maybe he was half crazy himself.

He had not told Ruth Rose he was coming to the *Expositor*. He wasn't sure he would help her. All he knew was that she had lit a fire inside him. Some kind of burning need to know.

He checked his watch. It was time to leave. But there was something else he needed to look up, while he was here. Plucking up his courage, he dug out the newspaper yearbook for 1997 and turned to September. With his heart pumping and a lump as big as a bullfrog in his throat, he turned the pages until he found the edition that featured his father's disappearance.

There was an out-of-focus photo on the front page of volunteers combing the Hawkins land for traces of the missing man. With a shaking finger he scanned the article for something he dimly remembered reading there. Then his finger landed and his eyes scanned the paragraph.

A buzz of excitement arose at one point early

on Friday afternoon when a searcher discovered a brand new lip balm dispenser in a deep thicket near the property line and far from any road or byway. As instructed, the searcher did not touch the article but reported the find to the nearest police officer. Sadly, it turned out that the discovery was a red herring. The lip balm belonged to one of the other volunteers who had wandered out of his prescribed search area. The searcher apologized for raising the team's hopes. It was Father Fisher of the Church of the Blessed Transfiguration, who was Hub Hawkins' pastor and friend.

Without a sound, Jim closed the heavy book and leaned against the sloping counter. Dorothy wandered by from the front office on her way to the print shop. He didn't acknowledge her smile. It crossed his mind that he must look lost in thought.

But he wasn't lost. For the first time in a year he felt he saw the faintest trace of a trail opening up before him.

7

Jim stepped out of the *Ladybank Expositor* building onto McMartin Street and stood for a moment stock-still. The sunlight — what there was left of it — made him blink after almost an hour in the stuffy, windowless corridor. He still had the smell of aging newsprint in his nose.

He took a deep breath — a good strong whiff of fall-cooled air and car fumes. His head was buzzing with strange images: a burning log cabin in a field of snow, flat irons dancing down a staircase, and a tiny little plastic dispenser of lip balm lying on the rotting floor of the forest. In his mind's eye the dispenser glowed like something lit from inside.

He heard his name and turned to see Hec Menzies at the door of the newspaper office, his glasses on his head.

"Didn't see you leave, Jimbo," he said. "Get what you were after?"

"I'm not sure," said Jim. "But, thanks."

"No problem. That's what a paper is for." Hec smiled at him but there were little searchlights in his eyes. "Working on a school project, are you?"

"No, sir," said Jim, his hand instinctively closing around the folded piece of foolscap in his pocket. "Just something I was interested in, that's all."

Hec nodded, rolled down his sleeves against the chill in the air.

"Well, glad to be of service," he said. He held out his hand. Jim shook it. The old man held on an extra second. "Good to see you back on your feet, Jimbo. If there's anything else you're after, don't hesitate to come around for another visit, you hear?"

"Promise," said Jim. Then he waved and turned along McMartin Street. As he turned left down Truelove towards the library, he saw that Hec was still standing in the doorway following him with his eyes.

It wasn't far to the library and there was still half an hour before his mother was to pick him up. Time enough to set himself up behind a wall of books and try to sort out the jumble of images in his head.

Ruth Rose had accused him of being afraid. "You're not ready for this," she had told him. Twice. Well, she had that right. But there was stuff Jim couldn't ignore no matter how hard he tried, and now it came elbowing its way into his brain.

For months before Hub went missing he had suffered from what the family called nerves and what the inquest called paranoid delusions. He believed someone or something was after him. Jim saw little evidence of the symptoms at the time; his father kept the worst from him. What Jim experienced was his father's long silences and longer walks and then moments of holding Jim in his arms too tightly and telling him how much he loved him. Iris begged Hub to see a doctor but he told her — and Jim did hear this — "I don't need a doctor to tell me what I already know." He prayed a lot, worked his farm and took his troubles to his spiritual advisor, Father Fisher. At the inquest Father spoke of Hub's delusional state, revealing no source for it beyond the "mysteries of the Lord's working."

If Ruth Rose was telling the truth, Father knew, all right, what was behind Hub's feelings of persecution. Somebody *had* been out to get him!

What had Ruth Rose overheard at the church the night before his father disappeared? *She's got nothing to go on.*

But who? Laverne Tufts?

A past was a big thing. Jim didn't want to jump to any conclusions. He knew hardly anything about his father's past. So why did he feel, suddenly, as if he knew far more than he ever wanted to know?

He crossed Truelove, and just as he reached the walk on the east side, a vehicle passed him and pulled into the next available parking spot up ahead.

It was the Godmobile.

Flustered, Jim pretended not to notice, but the driver's door opened and it was too late.

"Is that Jim Hawkins?" came the hearty voice of Father Fisher. "This has got to be the answer to a prayer."

The memory of what Ruth Rose had told Jim flashed through his mind and he was suddenly afraid the pastor might fall to his knees right there on Truelove Street. Instead he took both of Jim's hands warmly in his own, the way he did at the door of the church after Sunday service.

"How are you, son?" he asked, his grey eyes beaming. They were sharp eyes — little bits of Cambrian Shield granite set in a face that was surprisingly smooth and young for a man near fifty. He was the size of Jim's father and, like Hub Hawkins, he had grown up on a farm. Though he was now in the business of farming souls, as he liked to say, he still had a real farmer's stockiness about him — the rounded, muscular shoulders, broad chest and ham-sized hands. Unlike Hub, whose hair had thinned on top and gone to salt and pepper, Father Fisher's hair was lustrous and thick and raven black. It must be dyed, thought Jim. It was the first time such a thing had crossed his mind. And then he thought, if it was dyed, it was surely the only thing he had in common with his step-daughter.

"I'm fine, Father," said Jim. "How are you, sir?"

"Better for seeing you," said the minister. "We've been doing a mighty job of praying for you over at the Blessed T." He liked to call the church the Blessed T., as if it were a ranch and the parishioners were all cattle waiting for God's brand to be burned into their hearts. His homilies were always ripe with metaphors. Cattle sometimes, fish other times, needing to be schooled, lest the Devil shark gobble them all up. The children in the congregation would laugh out loud and the parents would chuckle and nod their heads in appreciation. He was a good storyteller.

He was still holding Jim's hands. It was odd, thought Jim, because it was the second time in less than five minutes that a grown-up had held onto him as if maybe he was going to slip away.

"Are you library bound?" he asked.

Jim nodded.

"Well, bless my soul, I was heading that way myself. They've got a new Colin Dexter on hold for me. Do you like mysteries, Jim?"

"Not much."

"I like a good mystery," said Father Fisher. "Mind if I tag along?"

"No, sir," said Jim. He had been flustered when he first saw him, but it was hard to keep Ruth Rose's loathing of the man in mind when you were in his presence. The pastor seemed almost ready to explode with good will.

They started walking and each time the pastor turned towards him to ask how his mother was doing, how school was going, his cross caught the light. It was roughly crafted but contained chips of a beautiful green crystalline stone. It dazzled Jim.

Then the minister said, "I gather you've been seeing something of Ruth Rose."

Jim answered, "Yes, sir," before he could stop himself. "I mean, I ran into her," he added quickly.

"God love us, she's something, isn't she?"

"Something?"

The minister chuckled. "I guess you'd have to say she was her own person. An original. I admire that."

They were almost at the library; Jim was counting the steps.

"She's full of fire," said Father Fisher. "Full of *passion*. That is surely God's gift to teenagers, isn't it, a fervent spirit."

Jim knew he had to say something. "She's pretty spirited, all right," he said. Then suddenly he felt as though he had betrayed her.

Father Fisher stopped walking. Out of politeness, Jim stopped, too. The minister was looking into the distance but not at anything Jim could see — his head tilted back a little to one side, like a man listening to some distant sound. It made Jim nervous.

"She's a troubled child, Jim," said Father Fisher. His voice had dropped. He spoke tenderly. "Did you sense that, son?"

"She seemed okay to me." Jim's eyes skittered away from contact. The minister turned to him, stepped between him and the library, blocking his way as if he could see Jim's impatience in his eyes.

"Jim, I'm not sure if it's my place to be telling you this, but I feel I owe it to you as a family friend." His voice dropped further still. "Young Ruth Rose has had a hard time of it. The death of her father has resulted in some severe psychotic episodes. Do you know what that means?"

Jim shook his head.

"It means that there are times when she loses it, as you might say. Misapprehends and misinterprets the true nature of reality."

Jim felt the hairs on the back of his head stand up. Father's voice was so sad and so persuasive that Jim suddenly felt every bruise the girl had dealt him in their first meeting. He could see her bared teeth as she pinned him to the ground.

"Are you okay, Jimbo?" Fisher asked.

Jim couldn't look at the pastor. He nodded. "I'm sorry," he muttered. "I mean, about Ruth Rose."

Father Fisher smiled at him and rested a fatherly hand on his shoulder.

"You've seen it happen, haven't you?" said the pastor. "Seen her fantasies get the best of her."

Jim glanced up at him and he wanted to nod vigorously — share with someone that first meeting in the woods. But somehow he managed to shake his head instead.

"No, sir," he said. "It sounds bad, though. Scary."

"It's a fiercesome sight," said Father Fisher, a sombre expression on his face. "It's chronic and that is tragic in one so young." He squeezed Jim's shoulder.

"I really am sorry," said Jim. Father Fisher let his hand drop.

"I'm sure you are," he said. "And I'm sure you will understand that one must be very careful with the girl. She's as smart as a whip, Jim. But the thing is, you see, she hears these voices. Voices whispering awful things, telling her to do awful things. I hope she didn't scare you?"

Before Jim knew what he was doing, he found himself nodding. Then he caught himself.

"Not really," he said. "I mean, she surprised me, I guess. But she didn't say anything weird or anything."

Jim was sure he saw relief in the pastor's eyes. "Good, I'm glad to hear that," said Father Fisher. "When she's on her medication, she can remain stable for considerable periods of time. But when an attack comes on...well, 'attack' just about sums it up."

His face distorted in a convulsion of grief. Then the expression passed and the minister fixed Jim with a weary smile. "She has been institutionalized," he said. "We really hope it doesn't come to that again." He sighed. "Poor Nancy."

Jim nodded again.

Father Fisher brought his hands together before him. "Each of us has his cross to bear," he said. Then his eyes got all dewy. "Jim, I hope, in the fullness of time — when you are ready — you'll join us again at the Blessed T. We miss your shining face, my son."

Jim looked down. "Thank you, sir."

Father Fisher grinned and held up his hands, as if for a benediction.

"No pressure," he said. "Just downright selfishness on my part. The ol' ranch just ain't the same without ya." There was a real tear in the pastor's eye almost as dazzling as the stones on his cross. He shook Jim's hand warmly and headed back up Truelove to the Godmobile.

O, Saviour victim, opening wide the gates of life to man below. That was the passage on the passenger-side door.

Father Fisher waved at Jim as he drove by. It took Jim a moment to realize that the pastor had forgotten all about the book he had on hold.

In the library, Jim went right up to the counter and asked Mrs. Bhanerjee if they had a new Colin Dexter. She punched the name in on her terminal, waited, shook her head. "Nothing since *Death Is Now My Neighbour*," she said.

"Is it on hold?" asked Jim.

Mrs. Bhanerjee checked and shook her head again. "I didn't know you liked mysteries, Jim."

A small smile lit up Jim's face. "I'm beginning to," he said.

8

There was construction on Highway 7. Jim and his mother had to sit in the truck and wait while earth-moving equipment lumbered across their path. The truck was idling funny. They both heard it — a clackety sound that could only mean repair bills some time soon.

"Did Father find you?" Iris Hawkins asked over the clacking.

"Find me?"

"I was talking to him earlier," she said. "I told him where you would be."

Jim was sitting knee-deep in groceries. He fidgeted. A carton of tea spilled out of a shopping bag. He tried to pick it up with his feet and put it back in the bag.

"That's weird," he said. "Father pretended he had been on his way to the library and it was a big surprise running into me."

Jim glanced at his mother. This didn't seem to strike her as relevant. Obviously she had something else on her mind.

"What did he want to talk about?" she asked.

Jim delved into a bag and found a box of Saltines. He opened it, helped himself to a couple.

"He just wanted to see how I was doing," he said. "You know, see if I was ready to come back."

His mother nodded. She looked as if she was going to say something but changed her mind. So Jim went on.

"Father said he was picking up this mystery they had reserved for him, but they didn't. I asked. They didn't even have the book at all."

Iris peered at Jim under lowered eyebrows. "What made you ask?

"Pardon?"

"Were you checking up on him?"

Jim shrugged. "It was kind of...peculiar." He was going to say suspicious but didn't want to get into that. With relief, he watched her turn on the radio. It didn't work so well with just a coat hanger for an aerial. She gave up after a minute and turned it off. The static had only deepened her frown.

"Why was it kind of peculiar?" she asked. There were little needles in her voice. Not anger, really, but something. Worry?

Jim kept his eyes on the earth mover, listened to its back-up beeping noise. "Well, it was sort of a white lie," he said. "I mean, why didn't he just say he'd been talking to you? Why did he make up anything at all?" Jim tried to keep his voice light.

His mother dismissed him with a little snort. "He's a busy man, Jim," she said. "I imagine his mind was on other things. He has parishioners to visit in hospital, folks who need his prayers."

"Yeah, I guess."

Outside, a girl in a hard hat and fluorescent yellow jacket swirled her sign from STOP to SLOW.

"You know about his Kosovo Relief Fund?" Iris asked, as she put the truck in gear and edged ahead. "I know that's taking up a huge part of his time right now."

"Yes, ma'am," said Jim. He had seen notices his mother had brought home from church.

"Do you know what he's done? He's gotten all the churches in Ladybank to work together on this. When did you ever hear of such a thing? All working together. Not only that, he's spoken to all the service clubs in town and even a couple of the factories." Her voice had risen a notch, as if this was a point she needed to make. "What started out as a gesture of compassion from our little congregation has now brought in something like thirty-seven thousand dollars! All because of the effort of one man. Do you have any idea how amazing that is?" She paused. "And the thing is, Jim, he does this kind of thing all the time. He is a very committed man."

Jim couldn't believe his tattle-tale had provoked such a lecture. It was clear to him that Father Fisher's character was not up for debate.

"You're right," he said as enthusiastically as he could. "It is pretty amazing, about the Kosovo fund. And the other stuff. I know it."

His mother nodded. They were finally able to pull back onto the highway. Two of the cars following them immediately pulled out to pass. The truck didn't accelerate all that fast.

"It's a miracle, Jimbo," said Iris Hawkins with a tremulousness in her voice that surprised him. He looked at her and she returned his glance with eyes full of fuss and worry, then quickly turned her attention back to the road. But Jim knew, suddenly, that Father Fisher had got to her. He must have told her about Jim's run-in with Ruth Rose, how sick the girl was with her demented campaign against her stepfather. That's why his mother was getting all hot under the collar.

He didn't want that. Didn't want her worrying about him.

Ruth Rose phoned him again that night. It was just after his mother had set off for work, as if she had been waiting. As if she had been watching.

"Can you talk?" she asked. Her voice was raised, almost shrill. There were street sounds behind her. It seemed she was phoning from a phone booth.

"What do you want?" he said guardedly. He looked out the window across the windy yard, half expecting to see a lit phone booth out on the Twelfth Line. Jim heard a car's horn beeping in the receiver, otherwise silence. He was just about to ask if she was still there when, at last, she spoke.

"I've figured it out," she said.

Jim pulled a chair out from the table and sat down. "Figured out what?"

"How he did it," she said. "The day he killed Hub."

Now it was Jim's turn to go silent.

If Ruth Rose had expected some kind of response, she didn't wait long for it. She hurried on. "The big thing was he had to make sure no one saw him. He couldn't take any chances. So what did he do? He put on your dad's clothes."

"What?"

"Before he ever set foot in the Malibu, he put on your dad's boots. Puts on your dad's Dodds & Erwin Feed & Seed cap. Everything. That way there would be no 'alien fibres' for those forensic people to find, no threads or footprints or whatever that didn't belong to your dad."

Jim could hardly breathe. It was like an obscene

phone call. And yet he couldn't quite bring himself to hang up.

"Go on."

There wasn't much encouragement in his voice, but it was enough to launch Ruth Rose again. "The way I figure it, they met somewhere else — somewhere no one was likely to see them. Then, when Father had finished him off, he put on your dad's stuff and drove the Malibu back to your place."

Jim could feel the bile rising in his throat.

"They were about the same size, right? About the same weight. Both of them were big, anyway. Father drives the Malibu back to your place. He's got gloves on so he doesn't leave any fingerprints. If anyone passes him on the road, he could lower his head and they'd just think it was Hub — his hair's covered by the ball cap. Your mother's at the church and you're at school — no one's going to see him. He drives down the lane all the way to the cedar grove. He leaves the car there, then he walks south towards the train tracks, leaving nice juicy footprints. Then he crosses the tracks and leaves some more prints, some more clues. It looks like he's heading for the quarry. Somebody drowned in that quarry a few years back. Right? He's making it look like your dad just wandered off to kill himself. From there Father makes his way back to his own car, making sure this time he doesn't leave *any* tracks. Takes off the boots, walks on rock — I don't know. Then he dumps Hub's clothes — burns them, probably — and drives home."

There was a note of breathless triumph in her voice as she reached the end of her story.

The whole thing was gross. Somehow Jim kept down his nausea.

"Putting on a dead man's clothes?" he said. "Driving around pretending to be an old friend you just bumped off?"

Ruth Rose met his scorn with her own. "You really think that would be such a big stretch for a man like Father?" she asked. "Every Sunday he eats the flesh of the Saviour and drinks His blood."

"You are disgusting," said Jim, his voice shaking.

"No," she said. "He is disgusting." There was a note of panic in her voice. "Jim, you've got to believe me."

"Who told you all this?" he said.

"What do you mean?"

"Did one of your *voices* tell you this?"

For a moment there were only street sounds. Then she spoke. "So he's been talking to you," she said. "I should have known he would."

"Listen..." said Jim softly.

But before he could continue, she burst out, "Yeah, I hear voices, all right. I already told you that. *His* voice, Jim. *Father's* voice. That's because I listen at his door. And if you heard it — heard the stuff he says — maybe you'd begin to understand."

"I want to understand," said Jim. "It's just..."

"Yeah, right," she said. He heard her sniffing. He wondered if she was crying but before he could find out, she hung up.

9

The Church of the Blessed Transfiguration was not grand, but it was big enough to require a public address system. It was not the kind of church that lavished attention on stained-glass windows or altar dressings or brass zibzobs or painted statues of Jesus. It was a modest church. A modest church with a very good public address system. That was the first thing Father Fisher bought when he became pastor. And the congregation was pleased because that way they could catch every word of his stirring sermons or his funny homilies full of memorable analogies. It was such a good public address system that it never squeaked or buzzed. It made the pastor's rich baritone voice sound like he was sitting right beside you, talking to you alone, which kept the children and their parents attentive.

Jim felt strange being back. He hadn't been to church since last Easter, and his Sunday clothes didn't fit so well anymore. He had grown a lot since then. He had grown a lot in the last week. Grown to realize that church might be a good place for him to go after all.

Folks at the church smiled and greeted him with sympathy-hands and condolence-eyes. But for all that, it was almost worth going just because of how happy it made his mother. She hadn't pushed him. She hadn't said anything more to him about the church helping them out financially and how nice it would be for him to return the favour.

What she didn't know was that he had his own reasons for showing up at the Blessed T. Something more than worship on his mind.

Ruth Rose had horrified him with her rendition of his father's death at the hands of Fisher. But no matter how deranged it sounded, he couldn't shake the vision from his head. It was as if he had been at sea for a year and she had thrown him this wrecked bit of flotsam, something to grab onto. He had no idea where it was carrying him but, somehow, she had stopped him from sinking.

However little Jim cared to believe what she had said, Fisher had lied to him. About a mystery book, about it being a coincidence that they had met outside the library, when the pastor had known Jim was going to be there all along. It wasn't much, but if he could lie about such things, then maybe he could lie about a tube of lip balm. He could say he lost it while on a search party in an area where he wasn't supposed to have been searching when, in fact, he might have lost it a lot earlier, walking away from Hub's car in the cedar grove, in Hub's clothes, just as Ruth Rose had said. Was she as crazy as Father made her sound?

The church filled up slowly. Organ music played in the background. There was no organ — the Blessed T. wasn't that kind of a church — but the very good P.A. system had a tape deck.

Tepid sunlight painted the pale church walls. Jim kept turning in his seat to see who was entering the church. Nancy Fisher arrived in her wheelchair, pushed by a member of the congregation. Jim stared at the door, hoping Ruth Rose might follow, the good daughter. Ha!

Her mother took her station beside the last pew by the wall, so as not to be in anybody's way. She was dressed in a colourful blouse and a bright blue pleated skirt. She looked cheery enough. She smiled a lot. People came over to say hello, and she chatted with each person in a nice subdued way, but as soon as they left, Jim noticed that her face fell and her eyes went neutral. There were pouches under her eyes, as if she didn't get much sleep. And her hands in her bright blue lap held onto each other tightly. Poor Nancy.

From the vestry at the back of the church the old sexton, Dickie Patterhew, appeared and turned off the organ music tape at the P.A. control panel. The congregation took their seats and stopped talking and then Father Fisher appeared from the vestry, in a cassock that was almost the same blue as his wife's skirt. He wore a starched white collar but, apart from his cross of glinty green rock, nothing fancy. Nothing to draw a person's attention from his smooth and handsome face and his neatly combed, lustrous black hair.

He began with a Bible reading. Everyone was supposed to be praying, but Jim noticed that a lot of the congregation glanced at the pastor. The people of the Blessed Transfiguration were so proud of him. He was the first home-grown boy to make it to pastor, and it was generally considered that he could have gone to a much larger parish in a much grander place. No, he had said. When God spoke to him, He told him he must stay right there amongst his people. The congregation was glad about that. And they were smug, too, because the other churches in town which were bigger and older and fancier didn't have a pastor who could hold a candle to their own Father Fisher when it came to preaching the word of the Lord. And no wonder. He was a man who had been saved from the fires of Hell and was thankful every day for his salvation.

Every child who grew up at the Blessed T. knew the story of how their pastor had been called to the sacred ministry. To Jim it had always sounded like a legend or something, and he had never questioned it. Just the way he had never really known that his dad and Father Fisher grew up together, right there on the Twelfth Line. It was as if the story told at church and the real story were cards in two separate piles. In the watery light filtering through the tall, plain windows of the church, with the farmer of souls leading his cattle in song and prayer, Jim sat and began, for the first time, to try to shuffle the deck together.

Fisher was the son of a shrewd and Godless farmer, so the legend had it. Wilfred Fisher had become rich capitalizing on the misfortunes of his neighbours. He had bought up half of North Blandford Township and young Eldon showed every sign of following in his father's money-grubbing ways. Gifted with money and a clever mind, he had gone off to university to study business administration and take over the Fisher empire. He had got as far as his final year with top honours. And that's when the Spirit of the Lord moved in him. The voice of the Lord spoke to him and told him to leave behind the ways of wickedness and go forth in the way of righteousness. And he had listened, forsaking his father's fortune and becoming a farmer of souls.

"We are all of us sinners," he was fond of saying. "And I am a great sinner, unworthy of God's love, worthy only of being trampled under His feet." He always sounded so proud saying that. God, it seemed, had shown compassion and had seen fit to shine His light upon him.

There was a picture that some child had drawn in Sunday school. It was part of the unofficial legend of Father Fisher, a comic strip showing Father wrestling with the Devil in a cave, the Devil overpowering him and laughing in his face, and God's finger lighting a nearby torch that Father Fisher could thrust into the face of the Devil.

The child had coloured it with pencil crayons. He had made the cave all shadowy and the devil fire-engine red. The fire had been yellow and orange and the Sunday schooler had broken his pencil making Father Fisher's hair black. The Sunday school teacher had urged the young artist to give it to the pastor. It was hanging in the basement meeting room even now, years later.

From what Jim knew, Fisher had lived just up the road from him. Jim had never seen Wilfred Fisher, the Godless capitalist of the story. They had never talked about him at home. Was he the Devil? Had Father actually fought with his own father? Who was to know? That was the problem with Sunday school stories. Who was to know which parts were real?

And what were the sins that made Father Fisher such a great sinner? Were they real sins or did he mean he was a bad person because he was just human, the son of Adam?

Father's voice suddenly cut into Jim's thoughts. He had mounted the pulpit and Dickie Patterhew, from his control station at the back of the church, had turned on the pulpit mike.

"Let us pray," said the pastor.

Everybody bowed their heads. But as Jim bowed his, he heard the sound of the entrance door opening. He turned to look.

It was her!

She was dressed all in black. Like a thief.

Jim glanced over to where Nancy Fisher was sitting in her corner. She had seen her daughter, too. For a moment her face lit up and then, just as quickly, she paled.

Jim's gaze returned to Ruth Rose. She was standing perfectly still, her head bowed, her hands folded in front of her. She looked humble, as if she were praying along with the rest of the congregation. But there was something in her hand. Something dark. For one horrible instant, Jim thought it was a gun. But it was too small.

Jim snapped his head back to look at the pastor. If Father had seen Ruth Rose, he showed no signs of it. And then Jim figured that from the pastor's angle up high, he probably couldn't see her under the lower roof of the narthex. Father Fisher's head was bent solemnly in prayer and his voice did not falter.

Jim dared to look back at Ruth Rose. She was sidling along the back wall of the church. Her mother was watching her intently with a frightened look in her eyes, her hands grasping the rims of her wheelchair.

What was going on?

Jim's mother touched his arm and gave him a look that he hadn't seen in years. It was a quit-squirming-around-in-your-seat look.

Jim faced the front again, but as the pastor finished his prayer and asked the congregation to please be seated for the sermon, Jim managed another quick glance towards the back. Ruth Rose was nowhere to be seen.

"The leaves are turning to glorious gold," began the pastor. "And we, Lord, call it fall."

Slowly, so as not to draw his mother's attention, Jim turned his head to the right until he could see Nancy Fisher. Her eyes were rivetted on something happening on the other side of the church.

Jim carefully returned his attention to the front, glanced at his mother to see if she was watching, and then very cautiously turned his head to the left until he could see all the way to the back. He could see Dickie the sexton, the only person in the back row. He was seated but his head was bowed in prayer. Or so it seemed. Upon further inspection, Jim was quite certain the sexton was dozing.

Behind him, Jim caught a glimpse of black. It was Ruth Rose. She must have ducked down behind the last pew.

"We see in the fallen leaves, the bare trees, the end of things. Death. But the Lord in His bounteous wisdom has seen fit to give busy Mother Nature a break. A nap. That's all. The beautiful maple isn't dead, it's just having a little snooze."

The members of the congregation chuckled and took the opportunity to make themselves more comfortable in their seats. In the resulting racket, Jim caught sight of Ruth Rose again. She had dashed behind the wooden podium that housed the controls of the public address system.

Suddenly he knew what he had seen in her hand. An audio tape.

His mother nudged him and frowned. Obediently, Jim looked towards the front.

"Come spring, as we all know, the sap will run

again. The gold of the fall will have been distilled. We will see it again, taste it again — and, oh, how sweet it is! — that golden syrup of which Lanark County is so justly famous. It is elixir. The elixir of rebirth."

Jim heard the sentence but there was something wrong. The sound had gone off. He was hearing Father Fisher's voice live. The pastor himself hadn't noticed yet. He went on sermonizing while all over the church people could be seen straining to hear, looking around, wondering what had gone wrong.

And then there was another sound, a hissing sound. And at last Father realized something was wrong. He tapped the mike. There was no sound, just the hissing that seemed to fill the church. Father Fisher strained to see the sexton who was snoring now, oblivious to the commotion.

Then the hissing was replaced by the sound of moaning. The congregation held its breath in hushed anticipation.

The moaning sounded like that of a grown man. What followed was unmistakably a grown man.

"O, God..." groaned the voice. "You have revealed Your great plans for me. And I am Your faithful servant. Help me, Lord, I beseech Thee. Keep at bay those who would stop me. Those who, filled with hatred, hound me."

"Dickie?" cried Father Fisher, straining to see the sexton. "What in tarnation is going on?"

The taped voice gave way to sobbing. "As Thy transfigured Son, Jesus Christ, commanded His disciples on the mountain to keep what they had seen to themselves, may my sins be something just between us, O, most merciful God, I humbly beg of You."

"Would somebody please wake Dickie," said

Father Fisher. But his other voice, on the tape, suddenly transformed into the voice of a youngster, and said, "Hub? Hub, it's okay, old buddy. Nobody ever, *ever* is gonna find out."

A baffled murmur went up from the congregation. Jim felt his mother gasp and tense all over. Father Fisher in the pulpit raised his voice.

"We seem to be having some technical difficulties," he said. A few people laughed nervously, and Father Fisher called out to his sexton, loudly, so that Jim, straining, couldn't catch the next bit of the tape. But he saw Father Fisher clutch the edge of the pulpit and lean out as if he was a sailor in the crow's nest who had just spotted an iceberg.

"Mr. Patterhew! For heaven's sake."

One of the church elders who had hurried to the back yelled out. "Hey, what do you think you're doing?"

At which point Jim saw Ruth Rose sprint for the door and barrel into the elder, who grabbed her and held her until she kneed him and he doubled over in pain.

The whole congregation cried out in astonishment. Jim, by now, was kneeling on the pew facing the back. He was astonished, too, but for a quite different reason. He couldn't believe her boldness. His mother's hand was gripping his arm but not to get him to turn around. She was hanging onto him for support. Her face was pale.

If you heard it — heard the stuff he says — maybe you'd begin to understand.

That's what Ruth Rose had said to him.

The tape stopped at last. And there was a sigh of relief from the congregation.

But somebody was not relieved. Nancy Fisher, alone in her wheelchair, suddenly let out a blood-curdling scream.

10

A flock of church ladies flapped and fluttered around Nancy Fisher. Jim stood up until his mother tugged him back down. Nancy, still blubbering, was wheeled out the front door of the church and around to the side entrance, where there was a ramp that led to the basement meeting hall.

Once Nancy had been wheeled off, attention swung around to her husband. He had come down from the pulpit and stood on the chancery steps, his hands folded together at the waist, watching the hubbub at the back of the church with a look of concern on his face. Jim wondered why he didn't go to his wife.

Then Dickie the sexton shuffled up to the front with Ruth Rose's tape and handed it to Father Fisher, who slipped it through a slit in the side of his cassock into his pants pocket. Dickie's head was bowed in disgrace. He had fallen asleep at the wheel and the good Church of the Blessed Transfiguration had foundered. Father Fisher patted him on the shoulder as if he were a child and sent him back to the control panel. Then the pastor climbed back into the pulpit. Every eye followed him up the stairs, watched him put his papers in order and tap the microphone to make sure that it was on again.

"Where was I," he said.

The congregation burst into nervous laughter. There was even a scattering of applause.

Jim didn't laugh; Jim didn't clap. Glancing sideways, he noticed that his mother was not laughing, either.

"In my humble home," continued Father, "I have a small corner, a room of my own, where I say my prayers. Praying, you see, is not only my day job."

Jim felt the congregation smile with pride at Father's recovery, the way he was turning the interruption around.

"Folks," said the pastor, "I take my work home with me. It is always unfinished. We are unfinished. Without the Lord to talk to, to bring our sins and sorrows to, we would be wretched beyond hope."

A few parishioners mumbled, "Amen."

Fisher looked regretful, repentant. "We all have our crosses to bear," he said. Jim saw a few chins quiver with emotion. Everybody was nodding. Jim wasn't sure if he meant Ruth Rose or Nancy or, maybe, someone else altogether. But Fisher was quick to make his point clear.

"My daughter needs so much. Needs attention in the worst way, as you have witnessed this morning. She needs us! Needs you and me and needs the Lord who has so much to give her if she could but open her heart to Him.

"And if she were here right now, I would say to her, Ruth Rose, if you want to hear some praying, sneak up to my door tonight, sneak up with your tape recorder and 'catch me out,' and you will hear me sob and whimper and, yes, moan. That moaning is the sound the door of the heart makes as it opens wide. It will be *your* name I will be uttering, *your* name I will

be drawing His attention to, *your* name I will be hon-
ouring in my secret prayers."

He went on for another ten or fifteen minutes,
folding the startling incident into the batter of his
sermon, as if it were a surprise ingredient, but one
that would only make the final dish all the more
tasty. He even managed to pour over his concoction
the golden maple syrup with which he had begun the
sermon.

Jim heard with half a mind. He was thinking of
Ruth Rose. She was crazy, all right, foolhardy, but she
was right about one thing. There was something in
Father Fisher's secret praying voice that was as guilty
as sin.

He looked for her at the beaver dam Monday and
again Tuesday. She wasn't there. He called out her
name.

"I want to talk!" he shouted to the woods.

The only response he got was the screeching of blue
jays and Gladys grinning at him with her crooked
smile.

Tuesday night, after his mother had gone to work,
he plucked up his courage and called Ruth Rose.
Father answered the phone and Jim hung up quickly.

Shopping day rolled around again and this time Jim
went to Ruth Rose's house. It was beside the church in
the east end of town. The train tracks, Ruth Rose Way,
passed by the foot of her garden. The Godmobile was
not around.

He waited, glancing nervously up and down the
quiet little street, afraid that at any moment the van
would appear. He knocked.

Finally the door opened and there was Nancy

Fisher. She looked at him but made no move to open the screen door. Her hair was neat, all in bubbly curls. She was wearing bright red trousers and another vibrant blouse. But her eyes looked washed out, vacant.

Jim opened the screen door. "Hello, Mrs. Fisher. I was looking for Ruth Rose."

He wasn't sure whether she recognized him or not. "She's gone."

Jim remembered Father Fisher's threat about sending her to an institution. "Gone where?"

Nancy shook her head. "Don't know."

"You mean she ran away?"

Nancy shrugged. "Can't say." Then she peered into Jim's eyes, and an idea seemed to flood her face. "Wait here," she said.

She turned her wheelchair around and rolled off down the hall into the darkness. There seemed to be no lights on anywhere.

Jim waited, growing more tense by the minute. The hallway smelled of furniture polish and fried onions. There was a cross on the wall above a small table with a bowl of colourful gourds. But there were no coats or keys or signs of anyone living there.

At one point Nancy reappeared at the end of the hall and wheeled across his vision into another room. He wondered if she had forgotten all about him.

"Mrs. Fisher?" he called out.

"Coming," she said. But she didn't. He suddenly wondered if she was phoning Father. He stepped back out onto the porch and stared up and down the block, ready to run.

"Here," she said, wheeling up behind him, startling him.

On her lap she carried a gym bag. She seemed to want him to take it.

"It's some things for her," she said. "I've been so blind," she added, as if that somehow explained anything.

Jim wasn't sure what to do. "I don't know where she is," he said. Nancy handed him the bag anyway. He took it. "I hardly know her," he added.

It was the first time he saw her smile. "Welcome to the club," she said.

At the library waiting for his mother, he opened the bag and looked inside. It was mostly underclothes and socks. But there was something rolled up in a piece of paper held with an elastic band. He opened it. There was a note, three twenty-dollar bills and a container of pills, a prescription in Ruth Rose's name for something called Diazepam. The note simply read, "I love you," and was signed, "Mom."

Jim's mother somehow didn't seem surprised when he placed the gym bag in the truck alongside the groceries and told her where he had picked it up. He told her about the note and the money and the pills.

"I tried to tell her I didn't know where Ruth Rose was," said Jim. His mother looked hard into his eyes, but he had nothing to hide and her eyes softened. She sighed as she turned on the ignition and the old truck shuddered to life.

"Poor Nancy," she said.

Jim lay in bed that night, unable to sleep. He kept listening for a knock at the door, a tap on the window. All he heard was the wind in the maples, the rattling of the window glass with every gust. Several times he crawled to the end of his bed and pulled back the curtains to stare out into the yard. They had never bothered with curtains before the media people started coming around. There were no neighbours, no one to spy on them.

There was no one out there now, as far as he could tell. He crawled back under his eiderdown. He found his mind drifting, going over what he had heard in church on Sunday, the tape of Father Fisher praying. He could still hear the voice in his head, so eerie, like someone in a trance. But some of the words seemed vaguely familiar.

As Thy transfigured Son, Jesus Christ, our Saviour, commanded His disciples on the mountain to keep what they had seen to themselves, may our secret sins be something just between us.

It was cold outside the covers; Jim didn't want to leave his bed. But curiosity got the better of him. He climbed out and made his way down the creaking stairs to the parlour. He flipped on a light, blinked in the brightness of it. In a corner by the front window stood a lectern with a large Bible sitting on it. The passage was somewhere in the synoptic gospels, he seemed to recall. It was a special passage for any parishioner of the Church of the Blessed Transfiguration. He flipped through Matthew, scanning the headings.

And there it was. Chapter Seventeen, the Transfiguration of Christ.

"And after six days Jesus taketh Peter, James, and John, his brother, and bringeth them up into a high mountain apart, and was transfigured before them: and His face did shine as the sun, and His raiments were white as the light."

The transfiguration was a story well known to Sunday schoolers at the Blessed T., for the church was dedicated to the mysterious happening on the mountain when God came down in a great bright cloud and told the disciples that Jesus was His Son and to listen to Him and do what He told them.

Jim thought about the passage. His father had read the Bible, a fair bit. He was interested in Biblical history, too, and he kept a few books, companion volumes, on a shelf near the lectern.

Jim turned there now. He took down a *Dictionary of Christian Lore and Legend*.

Suddenly the rooster crowed, startling him.

He went to the window, peeking out through the curtains towards the barn. It was a long way until morning. A floodlight illuminated the yard almost to the doors of the barn. The wind picked up and leaves danced but he saw nothing else move. The rooster crowed again.

"Stupid bird," Jim muttered to himself. His father had once told him that roosters dreamed of sunrise and that was why they sometimes crowed in the middle of the night. But the sound disturbed Jim. He flipped off the light and took the dictionary up to his bedroom, where he perused it by flashlight.

It didn't take long to discover what he was looking for, but it stunned him all the same. Another bit of the puzzle. He turned off his bedside light and lay there listening to the dark.

He closed his eyes and prayed she would come around. And into the darkness he whispered, "Ruth Rose, have I got news for you!"

11

The fall rains came, hard as sticks, churning up the front yard until it looked like a muddy battlefield. Leaves in soggy wavelets lapped against the steps of the farmhouse.

Jim went out into the rain with a sign he had made under his coat. He had wrapped the sign in a clear plastic bag. With safety pins he attached it to Gladys out at the dam. The sign read, "I know who Tabor is."

A week passed.

At church, Jim watched Father Fisher, watched his every move, half expecting to see clues drop off him like buttons. Or lip balm dispensers. After the service Jim lined up at the door and shook the pastor's hand. He looked into his eyes and came face to face with someone looking hard into his own eyes, and they were both looking for the same person.

The rain was so bad Monday afternoon that Everett pulled the bus over at the bottom of the cut road. He turned in his seat to look back at his only passenger.

"This is what you'd call raining cats and dogs, eh, Jimbo? Mind if we wait up a bit? I can't see a thing and I hate getting them cats and dogs smeared all over the undercarriage, know what I mean?"

Jim minded, all right, but what could he do? The windshield wipers could barely keep up with the downpour. Cats and dogs didn't begin to describe the deluge. More like beavers and bears.

On the floor of the bus lay a canary yellow notice with muddy shoe marks on it. Jim had one in his binder; all the kids were taking them home. It was about Father Fisher's Kosovo Relief Fund. They were going to adopt a town in that war-torn Serbian province, a town the size of Ladybank, a few kilometres northeast of Srbica where refugees were flooding. The title of the notice read, "From Ladybank to Ljivno."

Jim looked up and saw Everett leaning back in his chair reading the same notice. He was wagging his head. "And we think we've got problems, eh, Jimbo?"

Jim turned back to the window. Being stuck in the rain was one thing; getting caught up in a one-way conversation with Everett was another.

Suddenly he sat bolt upright in his seat. What was he thinking? Everett had grown up in these parts. And he was Father's age, more or less.

Jim got up and walked to the front, pretending that all he wanted to do was look out the windshield to check on the road. The hill up ahead — what he could see of it — looked more like a river.

He plunked himself down in the front seat. Everett smiled at him, folded up the notice and tucked it in his pocket.

"Hear they're nicknamin' it the Father Plan," he said.

Jim nodded. "Father Fisher sure gets himself involved, doesn't he? Was he always like that?"

Everett hooted. "Well, you could say that. But involved in what, would be the question."

"Like he was wild, kind of?"

"He was a real caution," said Everett. He whooped again, punched the horn to emphasize the point. Then he leaned towards Jim and whispered behind his hand, as if there was anyone to overhear. "Drinkin', carousin' — you name it. Wheelin' and dealin'. Always near the cow plop but never got his shoes soiled, if you know what I mean."

"So what changed him?"

Everett leaned back in his seat, scratched his belly. "I guess it was after the fire. The Tufts boy dyin'. You hear about that?" Jim nodded. "Fisher, he just dropped outa sight, eh. Gone. Next thing his drinkin' buddies hear he's in Ohio somewhere at theology school. Boy, did that get a few laughs. But people laughed out the other side of their face when he come back, a reg'lar sobersides with a dog collar to boot."

"Must have come as a shock," said Jim.

Everett nodded. "Oh, jeez, yeah. His father was fit to be tied. Oh, boy, Wilf Fisher. Now there was a piece of work, if I ever seen one."

"But the fire..." said Jim, sensing that he was losing Everett.

"Oh, the fire. Well, that was somethin' else. I chummed around with Stan Tufts a bit — Frankie's little brother — 'til they moved down to Brockville. He and I even wrote once or twice when they headed down to Mississippi. Pen pals, like. Baton Rouge. Hot down there, so I hear."

This was the trouble with Everett. He could keep his bus on the road, more or less, but not a conversation.

"She was following up on her Acadian roots, Laverne Tufts — except her maiden name was Roncelier, see — French. Never liked it here. So she left that old slug-a-bed Wendall Tufts in Brockville and highed off south with little Stanley. I guess after Frankie died..."

Jim saw his chance. "Why do you think Tuff...I mean, Frankie's...death tore up Father Fisher so much?"

Everett looked momentarily confused, as if he had lost the thread and couldn't find his way back. Then he flashed a snaggle-toothed smile.

"Well, they was as thick as thieves, lad. They and..." Everett's face clouded suddenly. His mouth had gotten away on him.

"They and my dad," said Jim.

Everett looked up the road, sniffed, pinched his nose with his fingers.

"I knew they hung out," said Jim, not wanting the tap turned off just yet.

"He was just a kid," Everett said at last. "Just taggin' along."

Jim primed the pump. "Frankie's death upset him a lot, too," he said.

Everett nodded thoughtfully, but then his memory uncovered something to smile about. "Old Wilf was pretty sore about it, that's for sure. He was wild as a rabid fox, let me tell you."

It took Jim a moment to remember that the abandoned cabin had been full of Wilfred Fisher's hay.

"'Course Wilf was mad most near all the time, except when he was buying somebody's farm out from underneath 'em. The only thing made him truly happy was lining his purse. Most everybody hated that man."

Jim was about to throw in the towel, but then Everett said, "Your daddy — now he hated Wilf Fisher somethin' awful."

"Hub?"

"Well, who could blame him? Everybody in the county kept a weather eye on that horse thief. But Hub..." He shook his head.

Hate was a word that was never heard in the Hawkins house. A word Jim's father had forbidden him to use. Jim had never heard his father utter hateful words about anything, or anybody.

"Why?" asked Jim, draping himself over his backpack. "Why did he hate Wilf? I mean, if he was thick with Fisher."

Everett glowered, staring out at the rain. "Same reason we all did," he said. "He tried to buy your grandaddy out when he was down. Old man Hawkins was just scraping by — this would be the late sixties. Your grandfather had made some bad loans, interest rates went sky high, and Wilf was just hanging around like a vulture waiting to gobble up the place." He snapped his fingers. Then he laughed. "Why, one time Hub come across Wilf on his tractor and Hub, he pelted that old crow with crabapples 'til the old man near crashed the thing." Everett let out a great guffaw of laughter.

"My dad?" said Jim incredulously.

"The same. I seen it. Me and Stanley. Oh, it was somethin' to behold." He laughed some more, his gut jiggling at the memory.

"Another time he stove in the windscreen on the old man's pick-up."

Jim sat back, limp with disbelief, shaking his head. From the corner of his eye, Everett noticed and looked sheepish.

"Oh, you mustn't think I'm sayin' anything bad about your pop, Jimbo. Why, I remember my own daddy sayin' that Hub Hawkins deserved a medal for showing some backbone, havin' some spunk. And he was just a lad, mind you. A bit hot-headed, a bit of what you'd call a firebrand, eh. Nothin' wrong with that in a young fella. No, sir."

Jim could see that Everett was afraid he might have offended him. "Phew!" he said, grinning. "My dad, the dragon slayer."

"You got 'er, Jimbo. And as fine a man as I ever met," said Everett. Then he decided it was time to move on, mudslide or no mudslide. With his tongue in his cheek, and his bushy eyebrows jutting out like twin visors, he let out the brake and steered the school bus out into the flood.

The engine was revving high, the wheels spun, the bus shimmied from side to side. Jim clutched the guard rail as they made their way through one turn and climbed into the next.

His father a hot-head, a firebrand. This wasn't what he had been looking for.

They pulled up finally to the stop sign at the Twelfth Line. Jim was pressing his face to the window, looking out the other side of the bus, not at his own land but at the fields that sloped down towards the old Tufts place, now nothing more than a grassy hummock. He could almost make it out through the fence-line trees, the wild grasses and the slanting rain. Or maybe he was just imagining it.

A log cabin converted to storage, filled with hay, consumed by flames. And a boy inside — a self-confessed fire-starter — stupid with drink, but maybe just sober enough to be hammering on the door, trying to get out.

Suddenly, the stench of the bus got to Jim: the airborne residue of lunch-pail fumes, stale farts and damp clothing. He felt like he was burning up, and there was a boy inside him hammering to get out into the air.

They turned west onto the flat and stopped at the end of his laneway.

"Thanks," said Jim.

"Don't you ever doubt your daddy was a good man," said Everett.

Jim didn't look at Everett. "I never did," he said.

"Give my best to your mother," said Everett. Then the doors opened and Jim stepped out into the rain.

12

Jim saw the light in the driveshed and headed directly there, shoulders hunched, head bowed under the downpour. He opened the shed door, only to find the place empty.

"Mom?" he called.

There was no answer, just the rain on the roof and the scurrying of mice in the walls. Paint fumes filled the air. The Malibu showed signs of Iris's touch-up work, red primer like blemishes on a yellow fruit. His father's prized possession; in fact, his father's only possession that wasn't entirely utilitarian. Jim had always hoped to drive it one day when he had his licence. But they couldn't afford to keep it.

And they couldn't afford to leave lights on, either, thought Jim. It wasn't like his mother to do that. He flipped off the switch. Slamming the shed door behind him, he stepped out into the yard. It was only then that he noticed the truck was gone.

A note on the kitchen table explained that Iris had gone to the feed store for a supplement the vet had recommended for the cows. A stew bubbled in the crockpot and fresh bread cooled on the counter. The fire in the woodstove was down. Jim was cold and wet. He sat down in the rocker, stroking Snoot, feeling sorry for himself.

Ruth Rose had thrown his life into a turmoil and then she had disappeared and left a vacuum behind her.

It was as if until she had come along he had been floating. He had gotten over the worst of his grief, gotten over the terror, the urges to kill himself and after that — floated. A balloon cut loose. Going to school, coming home from school — a pendulum swinging back and forth, wound up by food and sleep but with no momentum to change the course of his life.

Now his head was filled to bursting with conflicting thoughts, his heart with conflicting emotions.

Snoot played with the strings of his sweatshirt. He leaned his face towards her warm grey face and got swiped across the nose.

"Ow!" he said and threw her off his lap. She immediately curled up on the rug in front of the fire and started washing herself as if nothing had happened.

She had drawn blood. Jim licked his finger and touched his wounded nose. Then he got up with a sigh and went to get more firewood from the porch.

He loaded up until his muscles strained and he couldn't see where he was going. He had left the door ajar so that he wouldn't have to open it again with his hands full. The door slammed against the wall, driven by the wind.

Back in the kitchen, he dropped the logs into the wood box, opened the stove, fully opened the vent and made a tepee of kindling. He squatted, blowing on the embers until they glowed and the kindling caught. Then he watched as the flames wrapped their greedy hands around the dry offering.

He loved to watch fire. Didn't everybody? Or was he a pyromaniac, too?

A chair moved behind him. He turned casually,

expecting to see the kitten en route to the table.

Instead he saw Ruth Rose sitting, looking at him. She was waving a kitchen knife in front of her.

"Just listen to me," she said. "Don't do anything until you've heard me out."

"Nice to see you, too," he said.

He turned back to his task as if it was no big deal to have some soaking sneak sitting in your kitchen waving a weapon at you. From the wood box he found a couple of birch logs to throw into the good old Ashley heater. Suddenly everything became a lot warmer.

"You sure are quick," he said as he closed the stove door. "And quiet."

Compliments were the best weapons you could use on Ruth Rose. They threw her. She didn't seem quite sure what to do or say and that gave Jim the time he needed to look her over. Her hair was bedraggled, her jacket waterlogged, her jeans mud-splattered and her sneakers — her sneakers looked like they were made of clay.

"You look great," said Jim. "Where've you been?"

She snickered and put the knife down on the table. "I've been okay," she said in a breezy way. "I've got lots of places to stay."

"Ruth Rose Way?"

She looked unexpectedly pleased, as if she wasn't used to people listening to her, let alone remembering what she said.

"Yeah. There's a million places to hide."

Jim was looking at her closely. "Like our hay mow, for instance?"

She looked wary. "Did you know I was there?"

He clicked his tongue like a scolding teacher. "You

need help with detective work and then you act surprised when I do some detecting." He stepped closer and pulled some stringy hay from her hair. He held it up for her to see. "Bet it wasn't very warm."

She didn't answer.

"I slept out there once," he said. "I thought it would be cool. It was cool, all right. It was only August and I nearly froze."

"Yeah, well, then I don't need to tell you." Her face was wan, exhausted.

"Here." He led her over to the rocker where he stood like a chauffeur who had just opened the door to a limo. "The best seat in the house."

She didn't argue.

"Pee-ew!" he said, as she sat down.

"Shut up!" She pulled off her shoes and curled up in the chair. "So I've been living in a barn for a week. What do you expect?"

"It isn't the barn," said Jim. "It's the perfume trying to cover the barn."

She growled at him. "My daddy — my *real* daddy — gave me rose water for my seventh birthday. I've worn it ever since. Every single day."

A car drove by on the line and Ruth Rose jumped like a startled hare.

"It's all right," he said, checking the front window.

"When's your mother coming back?" Ruth Rose settled back in her chair, but with her filthy feet firmly on the ground.

"Her note says around five, but she won't mind. You can stay here if you want."

Ruth Rose's eyes narrowed. "What do you mean?"

"I mean you can stay here. Your mom even gave me some stuff of yours."

Ruth Rose was on her feet again and heading for the door.

"Wait!"

She didn't listen. She was on the porch and heading down the steps before she realized she had forgotten her shoes. She marched back into the kitchen and started trying to squeeze her foot into one of them. Muck poured out onto the rug.

"What's wrong with you?" demanded Jim. "We're not going to tell anyone you're here. Is that what you're worried about?"

She looked up. He could see she wanted to believe him.

"We were there — at church — when you did your thing. I think it was the bravest thing I ever saw in my life." She stopped putting on her shoe and looked at him. He had to make her believe in him.

"I've found out some stuff," he said. He expected her to ask what — he was dying to tell her. Then he realized she was shaking like a leaf.

He jumped up again. "Stay right here!" He ran out of the room into the front parlour, turned and came back. "I'm not phoning anyone or anything. There's only one phone and it's right over there." He pointed to the table. "Don't go anywhere."

Through the parlour, up the stairs, into the bathroom. He put the stopper in the tub and started running hot water. He read the instructions on some bath soap of his mother's and carefully measured a capful of the stuff into the gushing, steaming stream. The room immediately smelled of evening primrose. Perfect.

He raced around a bit more, getting towels and the bag Nancy Fisher had given him, all of which he left in the bathroom, and then he raced down to the kitchen, afraid all the time that she would be gone. But she was still there. Snoot had found her and was holding onto her.

"I ran you a really hot bath. If you still think I'm going to rat on you, you can take the phone in the tub."

Jim realized he had been shouting. Not angrily — he hoped it didn't sound angry. He was shouting from joy or tension or some other crazy thing. Shouting to use up some of the energy he had been storing while he waited for her to show up, half afraid she had disappeared forever. People did that.

She didn't take the phone. Jim made a salad as his mother had asked him to in her note. He cleaned up the mess Ruth Rose had left on the floor and then he set the table for three. He hadn't done that for a long time.

She came down just before five, her hair all stringy but clean and hay-free. She had dabbed on some of her rose water and it was sweet, no longer having to fight with the smell of cow manure. She was wearing a shapeless pair of worn brown cords that belonged to his mother and a turtleneck of her own. She had cinched the pants up tight around her skinny waist.

She went straight to the window to see if anyone was coming. Then she looked around as if she were disoriented, until Jim realized she was searching for her sneakers. He led her to the sink. Her sneakers were submerged in filthy water. He pulled them out and rubbed away the caked-on muck. Then, while she watched, he stuffed them full of newspaper and put them on a baking tray beside the woodstove.

"It's not a trap," he said. "Honest."

She smiled dully and sat down on the rocking chair, still without saying a word.

"There's stew," he said. The aroma filled the old kitchen. She looked at the crockpot, then looked at the table set for three.

"I can wait," she said, and her voice was like a little girl's voice, as if it had shrunk in the bath.

Jim looked at the clock, looked out the window expectantly. "We'll talk later when my mother's gone to work."

He looked hard at her. She nodded, slack-jawed. There was a kind of dreamy look on her face. At first he had thought it was just because she had washed away her heavy eye make-up, but suddenly he realized what it really was.

"Did you take one of your pills?"

Her head bobbed up and down. She held up her fingers in a peace sign.

"Two?"

She nodded again and grinned. It reminded Jim of Gladys. It made him mad, for some reason, as if it wasn't the real Ruth Rose. And it sure wasn't the same Ruth Rose who had stormed the Church of the Blessed Transfiguration. That was the comrade he was looking for.

"Listen," he said. "Don't tell my mother your theories about Father being a murderer. I don't think she's ready for that. But don't lie, either, if you can help it. Don't freak out, okay?"

"Why do you think I took my good-girl medicine?" said Ruth Rose.

Jim started to slice up the bread for supper. He wasn't doing such a good job of it. The pieces started out too thick and ended up way too thin.

Ruth Rose started to giggle.

"Shut up," he said, which only made her giggle more. Then he started laughing, too.

And that was how Iris Hawkins found them both. Laughing their heads off amidst the ruins of a freshly baked loaf of bread.

13

It had not occurred to Jim that there would be any question of Ruth Rose being sent away. Without ever having discussed the issue with his mother, Jim had somehow expected her to welcome Ruth Rose if she showed up at the farm. Father Fisher might have talked to Iris Hawkins, but she wasn't the kind of person who acted impulsively or assumed things without hearing the whole story.

That's what Jim thought. So when his mother's look of shock passed, only to be replaced by wary politeness, he was taken aback.

Watching Ruth Rose shake his mother's hand politely, he realized that taking her pills had been exactly the right thing for her to do. As opposed to pulling a knife or screaming obscenities, for instance.

Jim and Iris had not discussed the outburst at the church two Sundays earlier, but he had seen something in her eyes that had led him to believe she might be hearing the same things he was hearing, seeing the same things, wondering the same dark thoughts. When Father resumed the pulpit, she had watched him like a cat watching a bird in a tree. That, at least, was what Jim wanted to believe.

As they sat down to dinner together, Jim felt a little flame of confidence ignite inside him. Things are going to be all right, he told himself. He trusted his mother. He could see her warming to Ruth Rose. And amplifying his faith as sure as blowing on a fire were the words she said directly after grace. "Thank God, girl, you're safe."

They managed to get through dinner talking about bovine mastitis and how the broody hen was now sitting on more than a dozen eggs and looking pretty uncomfortable. Jim even answered his mother at length when she asked him how school had gone that day, though he avoided pulling out the canary yellow notice about the Father Plan.

But, finally, Iris Hawkins folded her strong, workworn hands under her chin, looked squarely at Ruth Rose and said, "What are your plans?"

Jim jumped in. "She can stay here, can't she?"

Iris ignored the interruption. She gazed steadily at their guest.

Ruth Rose glanced nervously at Jim, then down at the table and the plate she had polished clean.

"I can't go back to them," she said.

"Not even to Nancy?"

Ruth Rose shrugged. "Mom's okay, but she's cracking up."

Iris didn't say anything. She reached out and gently lifted Ruth Rose's chin so that the girl could see her smile. Ruth Rose seemed to take some courage from that, managing a little experimental smile herself.

Jim cleared the table. The kitchen was filled with the clicking of the stove and the dripping outside. The rain had stopped.

"We don't need to reach any decisions right this minute," said Iris. "Except, I'm going to have to let your mom know you're safe."

"No," snapped Ruth Rose. Then she looked glum. "You let her know and he'll be over like a shot."

Iris frowned. "Well, here's the deal. I tell Nancy. If Nancy wants to tell Father, that's her business."

Ruth Rose looked dubious. "You think she can keep anything from him?"

Iris bent forward to look into Ruth Rose's face, hidden behind her hair.

"How about this," she said gently. "I phone your mom when he's not there. That way, at least, she's got some time to think it over."

Ruth Rose looked up. She didn't look convinced. Iris looked at her watch; it was just after six.

"Tonight is Bible study night. Starts at seven," Iris said. "Your father won't be back home until nine or so. I'm willing to tell Nancy you're welcome to stay here for a bit, that you need some time to cool out, or whatever. What she does with the information is up to her, but at least she will have some time to think about it in peace. Does that seem fair?"

Ruth Rose's drugged-up eyes looked sad, as if maybe she found it hard to imagine her mother in any kind of peace. She shrugged, sighed.

"We can try it," she said. "But she'll tell him. And then I'm toast."

"Are you afraid they'll institutionalize you again?"

Jim didn't know his mother knew about that and couldn't believe she would bring it up. Ruth Rose looked offended.

"Is that what he tells people? It's so not true." Her head flopped back and she shook her unkempt hair. "That isn't what happened. I don't expect you to believe me," she said. "Nobody ever does."

"Try me."

Ruth Rose took a deep breath.

"When you get sent away to the funny farm it's because a doctor recommended it. Right? Usually more than one doctor. Well, no doctor saw me before I got shipped off. It was after I got arrested." She glanced at Jim.

"She broke into the church," he said. "Father had her arrested."

Iris nodded. "Go on."

"I was sent to what's called an RTC, which you've never heard of, I bet. Well, just look it up under "teen help" on the Net. It means Residential Treatment Centre. Safe Haven, this place was called. It was up near Arnprior and it was pretty much a jail, if you want to know. A jail for loud-mouthed brats. I wasn't charged with anything. No authorities — no doctor, no cops, nobody." She looked sulky. "The Safe Haven people came in the middle of the night for me. Right into my own home. I'm not kidding. Ask my mom."

She paused as if maybe Iris was going to phone right then. But they kept listening. Jim had been filling the sink with washing-up water. He turned off the tap.

"I wake up and there are three complete strangers standing in my bedroom. I don't know them and they're standing over me — a female nurse and two beefy guys in uniform. One's got a tattoo, like he's maybe an ex-biker or something. It's like a nightmare, but it's real. They get me up and pack my bags. I've never been so scared in my life. They give me a seda- tive — an injection, like in some movie. And there's my mother at the doorway sitting in her wheelchair in her nightie bawling her eyes out and Father praying on his knees. Then, poof! I'm outa there and outa their lives."

She stopped. She seemed to be struggling to tell them, struggling against the Diazepam gauze around every nerve bundle, struggling against the memory of being snatched. She glared at them, daring them to disbelieve her. What she saw seemed to give her enough confidence to go on.

"I was at Safe Haven for a month. It costs a fortune — I don't know where Father got the money. They treat you like dirt, intimidate you, humiliate you and it costs your parents hundreds of dollars a day. Cool, eh? And you can't get away. Not until you break."

Ruth Rose looked thoughtful for a moment. "So I broke," she said. Then she grinned suddenly. "There was me in little pieces all over the floor. 'Oh, I'm such a bad girl,' and 'Oh, sir,' this and 'Oh, ma'am,' that... and 'What chore should I do now...' At Safe Haven, they like it when you break. Except I kept all the pieces. And as soon as I got home, I put them back together again."

At 7:01, Ruth Rose made the call. Jim could hear her mother crying with relief.

Then Iris Hawkins took over. "Nancy, I really don't want to interfere," she said. "But maybe it would be a break for all of you if she stays here a while. She can help me with the chores — heaven knows we could use the help. That ought to keep her out of mischief." She glanced at Ruth Rose, winking.

Iris didn't need to do too much convincing. She did more listening than anything else and her expression changed as the conversation continued. She became grave. "Yes," she said. "I see...oh, my..."

Jim and Ruth Rose exchanged curious glances.

"But, why, Nancy?" Iris asked. "Why can't you tell me now?"

Nancy's voice grew louder, more agitated. Ruth Rose wanted the phone but Iris held her off. "Yes, I understand...I'm sorry. I didn't mean to...yes...yes, of course..." And then there was a long pause before she said, as gently as she could, "But, Nancy, in a way it is my business...I mean, if Ruth Rose is going to stay here." The voice at the other end of the line quieted again.

"Yes, that sounds like a good idea," said Iris. "No, I'm sure she'll understand."

It was maddening for Jim and Ruth Rose listening in, but eventually Iris hung up. Unfortunately, she was in no hurry to explain what was going on. She fingered her necklace. It was a slightly battered locket Hub had given her with his picture in it. She never took it off.

Finally, she took a deep breath and turned to her expectant audience.

"Well, the good news is that she's very glad you're here. I think, from the tone of her voice, that she is not going to tell Father. In fact, she recommends that you do not, under any circumstances, cross his path."

A grin played around the edges of Ruth Rose's serious face. "You mean no showing up at church?"

Jim laughed, but Iris didn't. The look in her eyes wiped the grin off Ruth Rose's face.

"Now that Nancy knows you're safe, she's going to go and stay with her mother in Tweed. She says you know the address and phone number." Ruth Rose nodded. Iris handed her a piece of chalk so she could write the number on the blackboard beside the phone.

"Somebody from the church is going to drive her down. She's been under severe mental strain worrying about you...and other things — she didn't explain — and she needs to get away."

Iris paused, chewed on her lip in consternation, then put her hands together as if finished.

"There was more," said Jim. "Stuff about something not being any of your business."

Iris's voice was calm, giving away nothing. "She's going to get in touch with us again when she's settled in."

There was more, Jim knew it, but he also knew his mother wasn't going to tell them.

"She's probably too afraid to say anything until she gets away from him," said Ruth Rose bitterly.

Iris sighed. "Please, girl," she said. "Have some faith. If not in the Almighty, at least in your mother."

Ruth Rose looked down again. "I'm sorry," she mumbled. Then, suddenly, she looked up and a strange light broke through the clouds in her eyes. "She's leaving him, isn't she?"

Iris frowned. "Not at all," she said. "Nothing of the kind." Her voice was impatient. "She needs time out. That's all. It happens. It's a very demanding job being the wife of a pastor, especially one as committed as Father."

"What's going on, Mom?" asked Jim.

His mother scruffled his hair. "I really don't know, son." She stood up, her hands on her hips. Then she glanced at her watch. It was time to get ready for work.

Ruth Rose didn't offer to help with the dishes, but she stayed in the kitchen, scooped up the kitten and sat by the fire while Jim worked. He was dying to tell her about what he had found, but he would wait until his mother left.

At eight forty-five, Iris Hawkins started down the stairs ready for work. She had just turned at the landing when she saw car headlights play across the staircase wall.

She hurried downstairs, arriving in the kitchen to find Jim and Ruth Rose staring out the front window as a van splashed to a stop. A van as black as the night, the scripture on its sides and on the plastic windfoil obliterated by mud.

14

Ruth Rose turned on Iris, seething with rage.

"See!" she said. But Jim grabbed her before his mother could respond and started hustling her out of the kitchen. They were on the stairs when he stopped.

"Your shoes!" he said in a horrified whisper and raced back to the kitchen. His mother met him at the doorway with the newspaper-stuffed sneakers and Ruth Rose's jacket. He grabbed them and took off again just as he heard heavy footfalls on the porch.

Ruth Rose met him at the bottom of the staircase. He tried to push her up the stairs but she held her ground.

"I want to hear," she whispered.

His mother was already opening the door to greet the pastor. There was nothing for it. The stairs of the old farmhouse creaked terribly. It was better to stay put.

Edging along the wall where the floor boards were quiet, they were able to slide behind the old couch. Jim was pretty certain his mother wouldn't invite Father into the parlour. She was on her way to work. Besides, the room was a mid-week disaster area.

Jim dared to peek around the edge of the couch. Framed by the doorway to the kitchen stood the pastor holding both his mother's hands in his, inclining his head towards her almost as if he were about to kiss her.

"Iris," he said, "What a ghastly night. Hope this isn't an inconvenience."

"Oh, Father," she said, her voice shaky. "It's always good to see you, but I was, actually, just heading out the door to work."

He stepped farther into the room, looking around, unbuttoning his coat as if he had every intention of staying. Iris stepped back but did not move from his path.

"Is something the matter?" he asked.

"No, it's just that my shift starts soon."

Father Fisher rested his hand on his chest, grasping the green stone cross that hung there. He bowed his head.

"How thoughtless of me," he said. "I do apologize. It's just that we — Nancy and I — we're so worried about Ruth Rose." He paused, took a deep breath. "I'm just not myself."

Jim turned to see Ruth Rose, her teeth bared like a cornered animal, but not about to go down without a fight. Her mother had caved in. He was here to get her.

But before Iris could spill the beans, Fisher said, "She's missing."

There was a pause while Iris digested the fact that Nancy could not have told him about the phone call.

"Still missing?" she said. "How awful for you."

Father Fisher looked at her. "So you had heard?"

Iris nodded. "The poor kid." And then she made a valiant attempt to change the subject. "I thought you had Bible studies tonight?"

Father Fisher seemed to perk up. "Ahhh," he said. "I'm going to take the fact that you know when the study session is as an indication that you might be considering rejoining us."

"The truth is, Father," said Iris in a hurry-up voice. "I can't really think about anything right now except getting to work on time."

"Of course," he said, backing up. "I know how important this job is to you. That's why I'm really pushing the finance committee to consider assuming the farm's mortgage."

Iris's voice faltered. "That's so kind," she managed to say. "Thank you."

"There are some, as you can imagine, who have a problem with it. That's why it's taken so long, God help us. But I've put forward a good argument. We collect, as well you know, a substantial amount of offerings earmarked for the church's mission overseas. And I have remonstrated — quite persuasively, I think — that charity truly begins at home. That while our own parishioners are in travail of one kind or another, we are simply not doing God's work."

Jim peeked again. Even from the back he could tell that his mother was wringing her hands.

"That's very thoughtful of you," she said, her voice humble.

"I've done what I can," said Father Fisher. "It's now up to the powers that be." He reached out and squeezed her arm. Iris flinched.

"You said you were here because of Ruth Rose."

Fisher put his hands together as if in prayer. "I've been driving around, beside myself with grief," he said. "I called off the study group. You cannot imagine...no, I take that back — if anyone can imagine,

I'm sure you can — just how Nancy is taking all of this. Anyway, I remembered Lettie Kitchen mentioning that she had seen Ruth Rose up this neck of the woods and I thought I might just drop by and see if by any chance you'd heard or seen anything of her."

It must have been hard, thought Jim, for his mother to do what she did next. She had always taught him to tell the truth. Now, as he watched, she stared Father Fisher right in the eyes and said, "I'll be sure to let Nancy know if I see her. You can count on that." It was only when she had said it that Jim realized she wasn't lying after all. She *had* told Nancy.

Father Fisher took another deep breath, held it in so that his chest puffed out as big as a rooster's, then let it out in a thin exhalation. He took Iris's hands again.

"Thank you, Iris," he said. "I know you will do the right thing." He turned and headed towards the door. "She means a lot to me."

It was all Jim could do to restrain Ruth Rose. Her fists were clenched. The effects of the tranquillizer had obviously worn off.

With relief, he heard the door close on Father. Listening hard through the rain, which had picked up again, Jim heard the Godmobile drive away. He poked his head up to make sure the coast was clear, then entered the kitchen.

Iris checked her watch, swore under her breath at how late it was getting, but picked up a thin phone book that hung from a string under the telephone. It was the Blessed T. book that listed all the parishioners. Her finger went down the list of names on the inside cover. They were the people who worked for the church: the secretary, the sexton, the deacon and the elders. Her finger stopped at the name of Clive

Stickley, the financial officer. She called his number.

"Clive? I'm sorry to be phoning so late. It's Iris Hawkins. Clive, this is a little delicate. I hope you won't think it prying or just plain rude." There was a long pause. "There's a rumour," she said. "I just have to check up on it." She took a breath. "I hear tell that the church might be considering a loan to help Jim and me out."

She waited, and what Clive had to say made her wither before Jim's eyes. "Thank you," she said. "Thank you so much." She looked at Jim and gave him a wistful smile. Clive had a little more to say before Iris, with many more thanks for his time and apologies for bothering him, hung up.

"Well?" said Jim.

"It's true," she said. "They *are* going to help us. They just decided." Then she held Jim tightly in her arms and rested her head on his shoulder.

He was glad. Of course he was glad. But it was not what he had expected to hear. And not, he realized, what his mother had expected to hear.

But if Jim was disconcerted by this startling series of events, it was obviously not half of what Ruth Rose was feeling. From his mother's embrace he saw her standing in the doorway to the parlour, her arms crossed tightly on her chest.

"I'm so happy for you," she said, but she didn't sound it.

"Thank you," said Iris, letting Jim go.

"Think nothing of it," said Ruth Rose. There were daggers in her eyes. "Can somebody tell me where to sleep?"

Iris looked disconcerted. "What's gotten into you?"

Ruth Rose cast her a withering look. "It's pretty easy to see," she said. "He's done it again."

"Done what?"

Jim took over. "Forget it, Mom. It can wait. You're going to be late for work."

Distractedly, Iris collected her raincoat and umbrella from the rack behind the door, but she didn't leave right away. She gave Jim a long, hard, inquiring look which he met steadily. Then she took Ruth Rose gently but firmly by the shoulders.

"Like I said, have a little faith."

Ruth Rose looked as if she was trying to summon up a sneer, but she didn't say a word. Jim gave his mother a quick hug and then she was gone, off into the blustery, wet night, already late for work. They locked the door behind her.

Usually Jim hated to see her leave, but not tonight. There was so much to talk over.

He led Ruth Rose to the parlour and sat her down. She didn't resist. The spirit seemed to have gone right out of her. But she perked up a little when he showed her the black-and-white photograph of the Three Musketeers.

She recognized Eldon Fisher right off. "Look at the slimy look on his face," she said. Jim hadn't thought of it as slimy; he had thought the boy looked confident. Now he kind of saw what she meant.

"Is this your father?" she asked, pointing to the youngest boy, the one whose skinny, shoeless, tanned legs dangled from the stoop.

"You recognize him?"

Ruth Rose shook her head. "Not really. I recognized his freckles."

Jim blushed. "This here is Frankie Tufts," he added, pointing at the boy with the white hair.

Then he took a big attention-getting breath. "I

know who Tabor is," he said. Ruth Rose glanced quickly at the photograph, as if maybe there had been a fourth person lurking in the window of the cabin, in the shadows. Meanwhile, Jim marched over to the Bible. It was open at Matthew, Chapter Seventeen. He read her the verses about the Transfiguration.

"Stop, stop," she said, cutting him off. "Spare me the scripture. I get the drift. This is what Father was going on about on the tape, about being on the mountain and everything."

Jim was smiling excitedly. "Exactly, but do you know what the name of the mountain was?" He didn't wait for an answer. "Mount Tabor," he said.

She looked perplexed.

"They don't mention it in the Bible, but I looked it up in a reference book."

"But it's in the Holy Land, right? What good is that?"

Jim sat down again. "I'm not sure. Except that I bet Tabor is a place, not a person. He blabbed about Tabor keeping his secret or something like that. Well, maybe he didn't mean a person. Maybe he meant some secret place."

"So where is it? It's not as if there are any mountains around here."

Jim felt let down. His breakthrough didn't seem like such a big deal anymore. North Blandford Township sat on the southerly fringe of the Cambrian Shield, the oldest mountain range in the world. But it had been millions of years since there had been anything like a peak in these parts. He already knew from consulting a survey map that there was no place, no hill, no poor man's mountain called Tabor nearby. Reluctantly, he admitted as much to Ruth Rose.

"Right," she said, rolling her eyes.

Trying not to be discouraged, he pulled out the foolscap copy of the story in the *Expositor*. He looked over her shoulder as she read, proud of his careful handwriting. When she had finished reading, she stared at Jim, her green eyes as big as moons.

"Now this is more like it. What did I tell you!"

Then he told her how the death of Frankie had affected his father, made him quit school. He told her what Everett had told him — about Eldon Fisher disappearing from town and then coming back a pastor. He stopped short of telling her about his father's hatred of Wilf Fisher.

Ruth Rose looked at the handwritten account of the fire.

"What do you think about the haunting stuff?" she asked. "I mean, doesn't it seem a little odd?"

Jim's eyes lit up. "Go on," he said.

"Well, here's a guy so stupid he'd go light somebody's barn on fire and come home stinking of gas when there's a cop staying at his place. A guy so stupid he ended up lighting himself on fire. How'd a guy like that ever come up with such a cool practical joke? Let alone pull it off." Ruth Rose looked at the photo again and poked the face of Eldon Fisher. "*He* thought of it," she declared.

Now it was Jim's turn to search the photo for the clues that had inspired such absolute certainty.

"The Fisher family were from up the valley," she said. "They came from Ireland. I've heard Father talk about this wake he was at when he was young, a real kegger of a funeral where the corpse is right there in the coffin, with the lid open so it doesn't have to miss any of the fun."

Jim laughed.

"It's true," said Ruth Rose. "Anyway, he says these guys at the wake rigged up the corpse so that it could really join in."

Jim looked dubious.

"With *strings*," said Ruth Rose. "They attached strings to the arms and head, whatever — like a puppet — and then ran the strings up through the ceiling some way or other, probably through the heat vent. Then, when everybody was dancing and singing and cross-eyed with booze, these guys slipped out of the room, went upstairs and started pulling on the strings, so that the corpse sat up in its coffin and started waving its hands around."

Jim could see it in his mind's eye. It sounded demented, all right. But then he had never been to an ordinary funeral, let alone a wake. There had been a memorial service for his father but there was no casket. No body at all.

"You mean the haunting at the Tufts place…the lids dancing around on the stove pots and the irons walking down the stairs — "

"Strings," said Ruth Rose. "And him pulling them, I bet." Then she looked soberly at Jim. "They must have all been in on it." There was a look of challenge in her eyes.

Jim nodded cautiously. His dad would have been twelve when that happened, just a couple of years younger than Jim was now. And Eldon Fisher would have been about the same age as Ruth Rose, with Tuffy somewhere in the middle. The Three Musketeers.

Jim himself wasn't the practical joker type and his father hadn't been, either. He wanted to tell her that, but the glinty lights in her eyes seemed to dare him to contradict her. Why did she have to make everything a contest of will? He had done all this research, but he wasn't even allowed to have an opinion. He turned away, tried not to be disappointed, angry.

"You don't want to believe it," she said.

"I'm thinking," he snapped.

And he was. Trying, at least, though she wasn't making it easy. His father had been the youngster of the group, just tagging along, like Everett had said. If he was involved in the haunting, that wasn't so bad. Except that it was because of the haunting that Francis was caught when he came home from starting the fire. So in a way, his father and Eldon were responsible for him being sent away to reform school.

Jim tried to imagine being sent away from home. How horrible it would be to feel responsible for someone else being sent away. No wonder his dad was so down when Francis Tuffy Tufts died. Down enough to quit school. It explained a lot. In fact...

Jim looked at Ruth Rose. "What if Tuffy got really bent out of shape — depressed — at reform school. Like he was pretty nuts to begin with, but being locked up pushed him over the edge. So he came back to make a point."

"Make a point?"

"Suicide," said Jim. "The fire, I mean. Like it was a statement or something. It was meant to make my dad and Eldon feel bad. Which it did, big time."

He looked at Ruth Rose for encouragement. But she had turned her attention back to the article. Her forehead was wrinkled in thought.

"Or," she said, "it wasn't suicide."

Her eyes locked on Jim's. "They say Francis Tufts

owned up to being the ghost when he got arrested. He didn't point the finger at anybody else. Which could mean one, he did it all by himself, which seems pretty unlikely; or two, he didn't rat on the others."

"Which would make them kind of owe him," said Jim.

"Right," said Ruth Rose. "You said your bus driver called Fisher a real wheeler-dealer. So what if he cut a deal with Tuffy? 'You take the fall and when you get out I'll make it worth your while?'"

Jim wrinkled his nose. "How would he do that?"

"He was rich, or at least his daddy was. Bet he promised him money or something. Maybe he was going to come into his inheritance when he graduated from college."

"I still don't get why Tuffy would go for it."

Ruth Rose looked exasperated, as if she were talking to an infant. "He was caught red-handed. He was going to jail anyway. So at least this way, he has something to look forward to. Except that when he gets out and comes back, Fisher tells him to beat it, or whatever. So Tuffy threatens to expose him — them, I mean, your daddy, too. Then, kazam! Tuffy goes up in flames. Pretty convenient."

"Murder?"

She shrugged, but there was a satisfied look on her face.

"So you're saying Fisher murdered Tuffy?"

Ruth Rose threw her head back against the couch. Jim was staring at her pale, thin neck when her head jerked forward again, and her eyes were filled with irritation.

"When are you gonna get it?" she said. "When are

you going to face facts? We're not just talking about Fisher, here, Jim."

The insinuation was unmistakable. Jim blew up.

"Bullshit!"

Suddenly, there was a crash from the kitchen.

They both jumped to their feet. Snoot dashed past them, her hair on end. Ruth Rose grabbed a broom that was leaning against the wall and held it like a pike staff. They waited for another sound — the floor to creak, something else to break, someone to speak.

Nothing.

Jim sneaked towards the door and peered into the kitchen. Some crockery lay broken on the floor by the sink, supper scraps scattered all around it. This was a mystery that didn't take much to solve.

Jim turned to Ruth Rose. "I'll need your weapon," he said, trying to keep his voice steady, though his eyes gave away his anger at her. She was sitting on the couch again with the broom across her lap. She looked shaken, all the swagger and dark suspicion drained from her eyes. He snatched the broom from her.

He swept up the damage and then spent some time stoking up the fire, not wanting to talk to her, wishing she had never shown up. It was as if she wanted to hurt him, wanted him to feel the way she felt. As if she was lighting a fuse and waiting for the explosion…

When he returned to the parlour, Ruth Rose was fast asleep on the couch. Jim almost wanted to shake her awake, but he knew it would be fruitless. She was all done in. It was a relief, really. He couldn't go through any more of this with her now. His father a murderer: the idea was absurd.

After a moment of just standing over her, watching

her, he found her a blanket. Then he took the seat across from her. It was piled with his mom's sewing stuff and clothes in need of repair. He moved them aside and sat staring at Ruth Rose in a stillness broken only by the pounding of his heart and the steady rainfall outside. Even in her sleep, Ruth Rose's face was creased in a frown.

The heat came in waves from the kitchen stove. Jim found himself drifting off, his mind a jumble. There were a lot of ways to read the few so-called facts. And you brought to the facts what you wanted — what you needed to believe.

"All we've got in this God-forsaken corner of the county is history." That's what his father used to say.

If only history would stay where it belonged, thought Jim. And with that sobering thought, he picked himself up, switched off the light and went up into the cold.

15

In Jim's dream, the Godmobile sailed into the farmyard without a sound, on a muddy lake of fall rain. And out of the car stepped Father Fisher, in his long black coat and with his black hat pulled low over his eyes, gliding towards the house, soundless and strong.

Then Ruth Rose was shaking Jim, shaking him hard.

"Wake up, wake up!"

Jim woke into the cold of his room with Ruth Rose sitting on the bed beside him.

"He's back!" she was saying, but it took him a moment to realize she meant for real.

He crawled to the end of his bed and peered through the curtains to see the van in the yard, its motor and lights off, the driver still sitting inside.

"What do we do?" asked Ruth Rose.

Jim got his robe from the back of the door. "I'll talk to him," he said.

"Are you crazy?"

Jim didn't feel crazy. He felt scared. But he didn't want her to see it. She followed him along the upstairs hall.

"Don't let him in," she whispered.

"Are *you* crazy?" he replied.

Something told him that meeting Father Fisher at the door was somehow a better plan than giving him the chance to break in.

"Stay up here," he said.

Descending the stairs, he peered through the landing window in time to see Father crossing the yard. By the time he reached the darkened kitchen, Father was knocking on the door.

"I know you're there, Jim," he was shouting. "It's an emergency, son."

Jim flipped on the light and stood as tall as he could, staring out at the shadowy figure on the porch.

"There you are," said the pastor. His voice grew friendlier. "I've got to talk to you."

Jim approached the door and turned on the porch light so he could see the man outside more clearly.

His coat was undone; his hat hid his eyes.

"I'm not allowed to let anyone in," said Jim.

Fisher rattled the doorknob. "Oh, come on, Jimbo, it's freezing out here." He made a big deal of wrapping his arms around himself, shivering and smiling in a familiar way.

"Not anyone."

Fisher held up his hand in a placating gesture. "I understand," he said. "Your mother is a sensible woman and such a precaution makes good sense. But listen to me, Jimbo —"

"Don't call me that," said Jim, surprising himself as much as he surprised Father Fisher. A convulsion of annoyance rippled across the man's bland face. It passed in an instant, but it was as if his mask had slipped a bit and Jim didn't like what he saw poking out from behind it. He stepped away from the door.

"Your mother is not being sensible about one thing, Jim. Ruth Rose is here."

"No," lied Jim without even the slightest compunction.

"Oh, please," said Father Fisher, making no attempt this time to hide his anger. "I *smelled* her, Jim. Her perfume. She was here when I came earlier. I'm always leery of people who wear too much perfume. It makes me wonder what kind of stink they are trying to cover up."

Jim rubbed the sleep from his eyes. There seemed to be some kind of stain on the lapel of Father Fisher's coat. Father noticed Jim's attention waver.

"Your mother lied to me, Jim," he said. "That saddens me."

"No, she didn't," said Jim, no longer caring what he said. "Ruth Rose was here, but she ran away."

Fisher looked exasperated. "When I arrived home, I found that my wife had also run away. I guess we've got ourselves some kind of epidemic. There was a note explaining how her mother had phoned and was ill. But, interestingly, when I checked Call Return on the telephone, I found that the last call had come not from her ailing mother, but from here."

"So what."

The pastor held up his hand and managed a patient smile. "There isn't time for games," he said. He took off his hat and pressed his face up near the glass. He rearranged the mask again into a church-door greeting. "She has stolen something, Jim. It's that simple. I'm not going to harm her, I swear."

"That isn't what she thinks." It was out before Jim could stop himself. He saw the lights go on in Father

Fisher's eyes. "That's why she ran away," he added. But Fisher wasn't fooled.

"This doesn't have anything to do with you, Jim," he said.

Jim looked at the clock on the wall — 3:00 AM. What could he want at three in the morning? He was drawn irresistibly towards the door, right up to the glass. This made Father smile even more confidently. But Jim was only examining his face. There was a cut, a bruise. Some kind of abrasion on his right cheek bone. His eye was half closed by swelling.

The pastor raised his hand to touch the injury. "I had a fall," he said and sighed. "Young man, it has been quite a night, let me tell you." He put his hands together. "Believe me, all I want is something of mine that Ruth Rose has taken. She can't possibly understand what it means, but I am sure she will have been quick to interpret it in the worst possible light. I must have it back, Jim. Please understand that."

Jim stood in stunned silence. Ruth Rose had shown him nothing. Was she holding out on him? It didn't make any sense. Slowly he shook his head. Then he gazed again at the pastor's face.

"Looks like you were in a fight, Father."

Fisher turned away to compose himself, but there was nothing he could do to hide his agitation.

"She is *sick*. I tried to explain that to you," he said. "That child you are harbouring is deluded. She has terrible, morbid fantasies."

Jim didn't want to listen. He concentrated on Father's wounds and something else. His cross was gone. The crucifix he always wore — had been wearing earlier that evening — was no longer around his neck.

"Her stories sound real, Jim — frighteningly real —

because she truly believes them. She doesn't mean to lie; she can't help it."

But Jim was distracted yet again. The rain had let up, the wind had stalled. And in the country quiet beyond the hectoring voice of the pastor, Jim thought he heard a noise a long way off.

Father Fisher rattled the doorknob again. "All right, all right," he said, his voice both tired and exasperated. "Do you think I don't know why she has come to you? There is a hole in your life, isn't there, Jim? The horrible mystery of your father's disappearance. And suddenly there is this girl who can supply a ready-made explanation. An explanation that nicely coincides with her favourite fantasy. And you fell for it."

Jim was shaking now.

"She's dangerous, Jim. You're afraid to open the door, but believe me, the lunatic is in there with you."

"Please go away," said Jim.

"Hub was my friend, Jim. You *know* that."

"Please!" Jim yelled it this time and he moved towards the phone. "I'm calling my mother." That was enough to silence the pastor, and in the silence came a sound from across the fields. Something coming.

Father Fisher heard the sound, too. Jim's heart leapt; he knew for sure now what it was. He raced to the door.

The cornfield dog.

Poochie came barking out of the night like a wild chunk of moonlight. He came straight towards the back porch, barking his fool head off. The pastor turned to face him, leaning his back against the door. There were scratches on his neck.

The dog stopped at the foot of the back stairs, his hackles bristling, his muzzle snarling.

Jim laughed. He couldn't help himself.

Fisher yelled at the dog.

Poochie stood his ground. He even bounded up the steps, snapping his jaws, making Fisher flinch.

"Get out of here! Go home." Fisher sidled along the porch to the wood pile and grabbed a piece of ironwood as thick as his wrist. The dog dashed away when Fisher threatened him, but came back for more. Fisher finally started edging away from the door down the length of the porch, his back against the brick wall, making his way towards the front yard. The dog raced after him, leaping at him.

Jim went to the front window and watched as the pastor walked in long strides towards the van, whirling around to ward off the dog that hounded his every step.

As the door of the van finally opened, a loud hallelujah escaped from Jim. "Way to go, Poochie," he yelled, spinning around in a pyjama victory dance. The pastor threw the ironwood at the dog, missing him, then he jumped into the van. The door slammed shut and the engine started, drowning out Poochie's noise.

Jim ran upstairs, calling Ruth Rose's name all the way.

"Did you see it?" he shouted from the landing, out of breath. "Did you see it?" He turned to look out the landing window.

The van had not moved. He climbed the last flight of stairs.

"Where are you?" he called.

She appeared from the darkened doorway of the spare bedroom. Behind her, he saw the curtains billow in. The window was wide open. Her eyes looked strange.

Everything Father had been telling Jim suddenly flooded his mind. Then he noticed that Ruth Rose was holding something silver between her lips.

"What is that?"

She held it up. "A dog whistle," she said.

"I didn't hear any whistle."

"Of course you didn't," she said. "You're not a dog. You didn't hear it when I called him out in the back field, either." Then she filled her cheeks and blew as hard as she could. Jim heard nothing, but out in the front yard Poochie went into a frenzy of howling.

"Brilliant!"

Then they tore into Jim's front room and pulled back the curtains. The van still had not moved. And as they watched, the engine was turned off.

"Get your clothes on," commanded Ruth Rose in a low voice. Jim grabbed his jeans from the floor and pulled them on over his pyjamas, grabbed his sneakers, didn't bother with his socks. Ruth Rose swore under her breath. Jim was on his knees feeling for his sweater under his bed. Then he heard the door of the van slam shut again.

When Jim joined Ruth Rose at the window, Father Fisher was opening the cargo door. He closed it and stood with a tire iron in his hand.

Poochie danced and barked just out of range of Fisher's raised hand. Then the pastor moved with a quickness that startled Jim, and the tire iron came down wickedly across the dog's back. Poochie yowled and bellied to the ground. Ruth Rose screamed.

Father Fisher straightened up, tall, and stared towards Jim's window as the dog slunk away into the darkness, yelping.

Jim grabbed Ruth Rose by the arm. "Let's get out

of here," he said and dragged her towards the stairs. But even as they reached the landing they heard the sound of the back door crashing open.

Jim swore. "He found the spare key," he said bitterly. Then he grabbed Ruth Rose and headed back upstairs.

"Children," boomed the voice of Father Fisher. "Enough of this foolishness."

16

At the far end of the upstairs hallway stood a door that led to a room above the kitchen. The Hawkins family called it the apartment. It was a spacious room with windows on three sides. There had been some thought a few years earlier of converting it into a granny flat for Hub's mother, but she had opted for a seniors' home, and the room was only used for storage now. Iris had stacked insulation against the door in an effort to keep the heating costs down. It made the door difficult to open.

"Help me!" Jim whispered. Ruth Rose immediately put her shoulder to the door and, after a few shoves, they were able to squeeze through. There was a latch on the inside. It wasn't much but it was something.

Yard light spilled into the crowded room, casting jumbly shadows. There were odd bits of furniture and cardboard boxes laden with junk. Sheets covered a dresser, a rocking chair, a sofa. Everything glowed a ghastly yellow. Ruth Rose began to pile things, as soundlessly as possible, against the door.

Father's voice drifted up from the first floor. "I can only be so patient," he said.

Jim was already at the front window of the apartment.

"We can climb out onto the porch roof," he whispered. He turned the latch on the top of the sash and heaved up. Nothing happened.

They heard the pastor on the stairs. "Ruth Rose, leave the poor boy alone. He's got problems enough of his own without you adding to them."

Jim heaved on the window again. It wouldn't budge. Ruth Rose shoved Jim out of the way and tried the window herself. He joined her and, straining with the effort, they both gave the window one last attempt. Nothing. It was painted shut.

"Over here," hissed Ruth Rose.

She made her way through the confusion to the unpainted west wall. There was a window there above the kitchen door. It opened easily. A blast of cold air made the sheets come to life. Dust swirled up from the floor like snow.

Jim ran to her side. "There's no roof out there."

Ruth Rose leaned out. Twelve feet below was the wood pile.

"It's so sad," came the intruder's voice, raised to find them out, wherever they were. "Everyone knows Ruth Rose is mentally unstable, but what a surprise it will be when they learn that Jim Hawkins is mad, too. Of course, there have been signs, haven't there, Jim? The suicide attempts. How worried your mother was. And now this. I suppose it runs in the family."

Jim froze. Ruth Rose stared wide-eyed at him. "Welcome to the club," she whispered. By now she was halfway out the window. She was barefoot.

"No!" said Jim, grabbing her arm. "You'll break your ankle."

"I'll hang from the ledge and just drop," she said, shinnying farther over the edge. He held onto her.

"It'll make this huge noise and he'll be on us like a shot."

Ruth Rose's eyes lit up. She scanned the room. Suddenly she was pushing Jim out of the way and rushing, silent as a ghost, to a ladder lying in the corner, an aluminium stepladder no taller than she was.

They heard footsteps outside the apartment door. "Just give me the letter," said a voice from the other side. "You hear me, Ruth Rose?"

"The ladder's not long enough," Jim whispered directly into Ruth Rose's ear.

Again she pushed him out of the way. He stumbled over a chair, which scraped on the floor.

The apartment door opened as much as the latch would allow, letting in hall light.

"The letter," said Father. "Give it to me and I'll go."

Ruth Rose met the question in Jim's eyes with a wide-eyed look of excitement. And then, to his utter disbelief, she spoke out. Loud enough for Father to hear.

"Jump!" she shouted.

She dropped the ladder out the window. It clattered onto the stoop below.

Father Fisher stopped pushing on the door. Meanwhile, Ruth Rose picked up a heavy box of old kitchen things. She hurled it out the window directly onto the wood pile, spilling the box's contents, which crashed and smashed and chimed.

Jim was horrified. But almost immediately he heard Fisher retreat and run back down the hall. In another moment he was clattering down the staircase.

Ruth Rose grabbed Jim by the hand and started towards the door. But he pulled her up short. "There's this old place at the end of the cornfield." He pointed west. "It's deserted."

She nodded impatiently. Then together they raced for the door. They ran down the hall and down the stairs. They had gotten as far as the landing, when they heard Fisher re-enter the house, slamming the door behind him.

"All right!" he yelled. "If this is how you want it!"

Ruth Rose froze in her tracks. Jim took over. He snapped the latch on the landing window and slid it up without a sound. He pushed Ruth Rose out. She hung from the ledge until her feet were only a few feet from the ground. She dropped, landing in a muddy garden plot below. Jim crawled out the window right after her. He could hear the pastor crossing the parlour floor, then he seemed to stumble. Snoot yowled.

"Out of my way!" Fisher bellowed.

"Nice work," thought Jim grimly. Then he hung by his right elbow from the outer ledge and, reaching up with his left hand, managed to pull the window closed behind him. Father Fisher was already on the staircase when Jim fell silently out of sight.

Ruth Rose was already gone. Turning, he saw her running low across the front yard. Was she crazy? Fisher would see her if he stopped to look. But Jim didn't dare call to her, let alone follow. He took off around the house, where it was dark. Across the back lawn he raced, diving for cover as he caught a glimpse of Father in the apartment window, faintly lit from behind. He had lost his hat and his hair stood out in spikes. He looked like Frankenstein's monster. Then he was gone from sight and Jim was up and running, slipping on the wet grass, falling, recovering. He ran through the orchard, kicking fallen apples as he raced, past the garden shed until at last he reached the fence.

He hopped it in a single bound and ran until the cornfield had swallowed him up.

"Jim, what a deadly mistake you're making," Fisher cried out at the night in his huge pulpit-voice. "If you only knew."

Jim ducked out of sight, but there was already an acre of corn between them. Catching his breath, he hid and listened.

"You'll live to regret this foolhardiness, Jim Hawkins," shouted Fisher.

Jim shuddered. The voice was as cold and threatening as the night.

There was a moon, but not so you could see its shape. Its light reached Jim through the seams of cloud cover.

He got to his feet but stood perfectly still. He was listening for a sound that wasn't just the wind fingering its way through the dry corn. A crazy girl, heading west as he had told her to. A wounded dog. A maniacal preacher.

Nothing.

Too shivering cold to listen any longer, he started towards Billy Bones' deserted shack. With every step, a little bit more of his fear drained away, replaced by an anger as hard as a stone. He gave himself up to visions of violent confrontation with Father Fisher — pushing him down the stairs, cracking him over the head with a two-by-four, making him hurt, the way *he* hurt. Seething with rage, he started to run, cursing under his breath and then out loud. He ran down a shimmering corridor of rustling corn higher than his head. He only hoped Ruth Rose was somewhere out here heading in the same direction.

17

Two towering white pines marked the western boundary of the Hawkins land. A million years ago, last November, Jim had climbed one of those trees to the top, intent on jumping to the next. It had been his last such folly.

Looking at the pines now, picked out by the bleak moonlight, it was hard to believe he had even contemplated it. They stood more than the length of three grown men apart. He never would have made it. He would have died trying.

Luckily, Billy Bones had intervened.

Down to the right of the trees, hard up against the split-rail fence that formed the property line, there appeared a dark smudge of bush, a windbreak. Behind it stood Billy Bones' ramshackle hut. Billy had saved Jim that snowy November day. Saved him from himself.

The door was not locked. There was no electricity but Jim would not have turned on the lights in any case. Even in the dark he could tell that no one had been here for a long time. A scurrying in the corner made him start, but it was not a human sound.

Jim stumbled to the woodstove and found a coffee can full of matches. He lit one. In the glow, he saw a plaster statue of a little black boy sitting on the table, fishing. He was almost white with dust.

There were lawn ornaments everywhere: deer and fawns, flamingos and a dwarf standing in the sink holding his belly and smiling.

Jim located newspapers and kindling. Fisher would not be able to see the smoke on such an overcast night.

The thought of any more running exhausted him. He lit another match, set it to the paper.

The firewood was right where he had left it. He had visited Billy Bones a few times, tended him when he got sick. And then one day, on his way here with a pot of soup, Jim saw an ambulance driving away. And that was that. The crazy old man had saved Jim's life but he couldn't return the favour.

He tried to remember Billy's face but he couldn't — only his eyes, lost and confused. There was just this poor house, a few sticks of furniture and a zoo of abandoned lawn ornaments. And there was this wood, waiting. Almost as if Jim had been expecting one day to come back.

He left the door open on the stove. The flames lit up the squalid room. Outside, the wind had picked up again. Rain in the branches of the windbreak splattered noisily onto the steel roof.

He dragged a foul-smelling blanket from Billy Bones' bed, wrapped himself in it and ventured out into the night as far as the road. He had hoped to see Ruth Rose, but it was difficult to see anything except the faint lights at his own place. It was too far away to tell if the van was still there.

Why had she run out front like that? What was she going to do? Puncture Fisher's tires? Smash in his windshield? Probably. Some dumb and dangerous act of vengeance. How could anyone so smart be so reckless?

Suddenly the rain picked up and he ran for shelter back to Billy Bones'.

He fed the fire and felt its warmth melting the shards of ice in his bones. Time passed and, despite his best efforts, he drifted off.

Suddenly there was a hand on his shoulder. He jumped and spun around. His feet became tangled in his blanket and he crashed to the floor. When he freed himself, Ruth Rose was standing there. Sopping wet, white as a ghost, but smiling.

"Mind if I sit down?" she said.

Jim got to his feet, feeling like a fool.

"Where were you?" he demanded. "What took you so long?"

"I hid in the barn."

"Why didn't you come here like I told you?"

She glared at him. "Stop yelling at me."

He hadn't meant to yell. It was just nerves. He turned his attention to the fire, fed it and stoked it. Then he dragged more blankets from Billy Bones' bed to wrap her up. He pulled another chair over to the fire, shook the mouse droppings off it and sat down beside her.

That's when he noticed her bare feet. They were scraped and filthy with mud; one of them was smeared with blood.

"I had to wait him out," she said.

Jim went to the sink and worked the old pump. It strained and squealed but no water came. It had lost its prime. He found a rag that may once have been a dishcloth. He banged it against the counter a couple of times to shake the dust off it. Outside the door, he dipped it into a rusty bucket filled with rainwater. It would have to do.

He returned to the stove and kneeled at Ruth Rose's feet, dabbing at the caked mud and blood. She leaned back in her chair and tried not to flinch. He worked away as gently as he could, the fire warming his back.

When he next looked up, Ruth Rose was gazing behind her.

"There's a dwarf in the sink," she said.

Jim nodded. "Happy."

"I guess so," said Ruth Rose. "Except for my foot."

"No, I meant the dwarf," said Jim. "It's Happy. You know, from Snow White."

Ruth Rose sniggered. "Well, this place could use Snow White," she said. Then they both broke down in a giddy giggling fit, made worse by the attempt to stifle it. The laughter subsided in the dark and was replaced by a low groan from Ruth Rose.

Jim found her a plastic lamb to rest her foot on.

"I wonder how Poochie is," she said.

Jim thought of the dog. It had squealed, all right, but it had run away under its own steam. It was probably off somewhere licking its wounds.

"He'll be okay," he said. "That dog's tough."

"Yeah. A killer."

Jim thought again of the lightning speed, the viciousness, with which Fisher had lashed out at the animal.

"You could call him," he said.

Ruth Rose dug the whistle from her pants pocket. Then she put it away again.

"Dog might lead him here," she said.

Jim nodded. How could he have been so stupid? But then, it was hard to think like this, like a fugitive.

He got to his feet. He had done about as much as he could for Ruth Rose without iodine and clean bandages. He kicked at the floor.

"I hate this," he said. "I hate *him*."

"At last," said Ruth Rose.

They were quiet again. Ruth Rose leaned forward so that her face glowed red in the firelight. Jim cleared his throat.

"Why did you go out front?" he said. "You were a sitting duck."

She shrugged. "I thought maybe I could steal his car, leave him stranded. I know how to drive. Except he didn't leave the keys."

"Oh," said Jim. It wasn't what he had thought at all. He was all churned up inside.

"It was dangerous," he said. "Stupid."

"What is with you, anyway?"

Jim didn't speak for a moment. Then he steadied himself so that his words came out clear and unwavering.

"My dad never hurt anyone. Never. Just so you know."

He didn't dare look at her, didn't want to see the disdain in her eyes.

She didn't reply. The moment lengthened.

The rain beat down deafeningly. Jim fed the fire and it grew so hot that he dropped the scratchy blanket from his shoulders. He tried to guess what time it was, thought about checking the road again but only got as far as the door. The rain was a solid curtain. He returned to his chair but he couldn't sit. He couldn't stand the tension.

"What was he saying about a letter?"

"How should I know," said Ruth Rose, her voice full of mustard.

"He said you stole it."

"Who do you want to believe, him or me?"

Jim could feel her eyes on him but he couldn't meet her gaze.

"Okay, I'm sorry," he snapped. He glanced at her. She turned away. But then she spoke anyway.

"What I think is that one of the letters got lost or something — intercepted, maybe. Maybe whoever is blackmailing him got pissed off when they didn't hear back. So he figures it must have been me."

"If it wasn't you, who was it?"

Ruth Rose shook her head. "That's what I want to know."

Jim tried to think but he was growing more and more sleepy. He closed his eyes and there was Father Fisher standing on the other side of the kitchen door looking in at him.

Jim's eyes snapped open again. He hadn't even had the chance to tell her.

"I think he had been in a fight," he said. He told Ruth Rose about the cut on Father's cheek, the stain on his lapel, the scratches on the back of his neck, the missing cross.

"He never goes anywhere without that thing. It's like his good luck charm or something," she said excitedly. "They must be closing in. He must have escaped some kind of a trap. That's why he was acting like a cornered rat. He's close to breaking."

Jim looked at her. Despite her pain, her exhaustion, she was gloating, her eyes brimming over with fury. It was scary.

"We were lucky," he said.

"It isn't luck," she answered, her face contorting into nastiness. "Hate is a powerful weapon, Jim. Hate got me this far. I'm not gonna quit now."

Jim poked at the fire with a stick. He didn't like the

look on her face, didn't feel right. His brain hurt. He hurt all over. The stick he was using burst into flames. He shoved it into the fire.

He slumped in his chair, plumped up his blankets into a pillow.

"I'll keep first watch," he said. Ruth Rose didn't answer. She had fallen asleep. "I'll wake you," he mumbled. But he never did. He was asleep himself before the next squall hit. The rain thundered down, the wind shook the house so that the windows rattled in their casements. The door flew open. Neither of them noticed.

18

What there was of dawn finally pierced the grimy windows to give shape to the decrepit interior of Billy Bones' shack. It looked even more wretched in the dim light than it had in the dark. Ruth Rose found a pair of gumboots and shook the spiders out of them. Her foot had stopped bleeding. They had wrapped it up in strips of torn bedsheet. It was painful but she could walk.

"What if he's still there?" she said, hobbling towards the door, following Jim. Jim stopped, dopey with sleep. He hadn't really thought about it.

Ruth Rose picked up a lawn ornament. "We could flamingo him to death," she said. Jim smiled. It was good to hear her crack a joke.

They walked cautiously out to the road. As far as they could tell, there was no car in Jim's yard. It was cold enough that they could see their breath blossoming out from their mouths. They didn't speak, just tried to keep their tired eyes open as best they could and one foot moving in front of the next.

Ruth Rose kept checking behind them. She wasn't armed with a flamingo anymore, but Jim had seen her wrap a rusty kitchen knife in newspaper and shove it down her boot. He hadn't said anything.

The sun was lost to them, the palest pencil line of

light along a ridge that jutted up from a dark mantle of fir trees to the north of the Twelfth Line.

"What do they call that place?" asked Ruth Rose.

Jim followed her gaze. "The ridge, you mean?" She nodded. He thought a minute, racked his brain. "I think they call it the ridge," he said.

"Sure are imaginative up this way."

Jim turned his gaze to the hill. It formed an impressive backdrop to the gouged-out moonscape of Purvis Poole's sand pit. The pit was closed down, had been for years. Jim had never ventured much beyond it. He had played there sometimes when he was younger — the biggest sandbox in the county — leaping off the grassy lip and tumbling down, down, down.

He looked at Ruth Rose. Her eyes were fixed on the ridge. The highest point of land in the area.

"Are you thinking what I'm thinking?" he asked.

She cocked an eyebrow. "Mount Tabor?"

He nodded. "Maybe Fisher named it that."

"Did the search parties get up that way?"

Jim thought a bit. He remembered seeing the police helicopter flying low. But really the police had concentrated the search where they had found the car, down at the southeast corner of the Hawkins farm and south from there towards the quarry. He stopped in his tracks.

"Holy smoke," he said as the truth dawned on him. "What?"

"The clues," he said. "The footprints and everything. They all led the search party away from the ridge. The exact opposite direction."

Ruth Rose snapped her head in the direction of the high ground. They stood in the middle of the road and watched the light creep over the rim of the ridge and seep like pale lava down the edges into the trees.

"Now we're getting somewhere," she said.

There were no surprises waiting for them in the farmyard. The Godmobile was gone. Fisher could be hiding, waiting. Somehow Jim didn't think so. Maybe it was the ragged light of day or the prospect of his mother arriving home soon. Whatever the reason, he was willing to take his chances.

The back door was hanging open. Jim stepped into the kitchen but stopped on the threshold and gasped.

He saw the table on its back, a broken chair lying in the corner. He saw smashed dishes and torn curtains, and red. Everywhere red. Primer-paint red.

FATHER KILLED HUB

Three words spray-painted like splattered blood on the wall, the floor, the fridge.

He felt Ruth Rose's hand on his arm. He slapped it away and turned on her, breathing hard, dizzy with rage.

Ruth Rose met his gaze, her mouth gaping.

"Thought you'd steal his car," shouted Jim.

"What are you talking about?"

His arm flung out and pointed behind him to the kitchen. His eyes blazed with betrayal. "Hid in the barn," he shouted. "Waited him out."

Her eyes retreated into angry slits. "You think I did this?"

He didn't speak. His face said it all.

Neither of them moved. Then Ruth Rose stepped into the room and looked around at the ugly lettering, the ugly revelation scrawled everywhere, the empty spray tins, the derangement of what had once been a spotless country kitchen, and she laughed. It was the laughter of a mad person.

"Shut up!" yelled Jim, his face burning, his neck muscles standing out like cables. "Shut up!" he screamed, his voice shattering into a thousand pieces.

"You don't get it, do you," she spat at him.

"Oh, I get it, all right!"

"No, you don't. You can't. He's brilliant, Jim."

"What's that got to do with anything?"

She stared at him, shaking her head. Then she scanned the room, looking for something. She marched through the kitchen and into the parlour, barely limping now. Behind the couch, where they had hidden the night before, she found her sneakers and her jacket. She kicked off Billy Bones' boots. The knife tumbled out of its paper wrapping. She tore off her makeshift bandage, pulled on her shoes, her jacket, and then marched back through the kitchen.

Jim grabbed her as she passed; she shook him off.

"You're staying," he growled, his voice gravel.

"Oh, sure!" she said spitefully, thwacking his hand away. She looked around. "Hey, Jim, you've gotta admit. This is a great idea."

"You're a lunatic!" he shouted. He grabbed at her again, cuffed her, and she cuffed him back.

"Come on, Jimbo!" she spat. "It's just *perfect*." She pounded him on the chest with both fists. "Perfect, perfect, perfect!"

He wanted to kill her, but, even wounded, she was way too strong for him. She flung him to the floor. Then she fled. He clambered to his feet, took off after her, but as he stepped through the doorway, a rotten apple smashed on the wall beside him.

"Thanks for nothing, idiot!" she bellowed from the garden. She hurled another apple, which didn't make it as far as the porch. Then she took off through the orchard. She wasn't limping anymore.

19

J im didn't move. He stood in the centre of the kitchen until the room stopped spinning. The anger in
him subsided, but it did not go away. It dispersed
into every limb, every cell, every part of him now.

Looking down, he saw that he was standing on his
father's name. Huge sobs burst from him. The tears
coursed down his face and he made no attempt to
wipe them away.

He took a deep breath and headed towards the
counter, walking like a zombie. In the cupboard
under the sink he found some scouring pads. He
found a bucket and filled it. On his knees, he started
scrubbing away at FATHER, at KILLED, at HUB.
But the paint, as viscous as drying blood, only
smeared horribly. He sobbed and scrubbed and the
tears fell again, but not enough tears to wipe away
the mess Ruth Rose had left behind.

He was still on his knees when his mother arrived
home. She dropped what she was carrying. In a flash,
she was on the floor beside him, cradling him in her
arms as if he were a small child. She smelled of soap.
She had spent the night stirring it or cutting it into
bars or whatever it was she did. But for once the heavy
perfume wafting off her skin and clothes didn't make
him sick. Her own tears joined his. She looked around

at the mayhem, the gory graffiti and leaned on him for support as much as he leaned on her.

Finally he pulled away, rubbed his eyes on his sleeve, sniffed and crawled to his feet. His mother picked up a chair and set it at the table. She led him there, then found the kettle — it had been hurled into the wood box. She filled it at the sink. Sniffing, she put the kettle on the stove, turned it on, found the teapot — mercifully unbroken — and went about making tea.

The comforting sounds helped to bring Jim around.

"I'm so sorry," he said.

"It isn't your fault."

"It is so! I brought her here."

"You took her in," said his mother. "That was the right thing to do."

"No," he said, shaking his head. "It was stupid, stupid, stupid. I hate her. *Hate* her."

He heard the intake of breath, but the rebuke didn't come. She brought him tea with extra sugar, instead. They sat for a long time, letting the drink calm them down.

When his mother spoke again, there was only hurt in her voice.

"Why would she do this?"

Jim shook his head pathetically. "I don't know. I just don't get it."

After another moment she went to use the phone. It was dead. The line had been torn from the wall. She glanced at the blackboard. Nancy Fisher's phone number in Tweed had been erased.

Iris sighed. "Where is she now?"

"She's gone," said Jim.

"You only did what you thought was right. I should have known better."

Jim sat up. He suddenly realized that his mother knew nothing of what had happened during the night.

"It was because he came back. Father, I mean."

Iris looked startled. "Last night?"

Jim nodded. "Around three. He knew she was here. When he talked to you, he knew it. Mom, he came inside. I locked the door, like always. He just got the key from the porch and walked in."

Iris looked aghast. "Did he hurt her?"

"He didn't get a chance," said Jim. "We split."

Iris looked around at the devastation. "Where were you when this happened?"

Jim's face fell. "We got separated," he said. "We climbed out a window and took off. I went to Billy's place. I didn't see her for...I don't know...hours, I guess." He shook his head, trying to kick-start his brain. He looked up again, looked around him, his eyes opened wide. "I can't believe it."

His mother sat back in her chair, her arms hanging limply by her side. "Jim," she said, "Ruth Rose is a sick girl."

He nodded and hated himself for agreeing with her. But what could he do? She was sick. Twisted. Deranged.

Hey, Jim, you gotta admit. This is a great idea.

"She was right about one thing," he said. "I'm an idiot."

"Jim, stop blaming yourself. Bringing her home was the Christian thing to do."

"What does that mean anymore?" he said. "Was it Christian of Father Fisher to come here at three in the morning and scare us to death? Was it Christian of him to drive me out of my own house? Ruth Rose is crazy — okay, I know that now for sure. But I know what made her that way. Him. He's just as crazy and

I hate him," he said. "I hate them both."

With what patience she could muster, his mother spoke. "You know you are not to use that word in this house."

"Why not!" said Jim darkly. "I'm supposed to tell the truth, aren't I?"

"Jim Hawkins, please."

But Jim couldn't stop. "Right, I forgot. Because Dad hated someone and regretted it, I'm not allowed to hate anyone. Great. That's really fair."

His mother's face went ashen, then grew stern. "Did she tell you that?"

"No," he said. "But it's true, isn't it? Dad hated Wilfred Fisher. Well, I hate his son. Maybe it's hereditary."

Iris leaned her elbows on the table, let her head fall into her hands, too weary to fight anymore.

Jim looked over at her feet. She was still in her rainboots. She never wore outdoor shoes in the house. Nothing was as it should be. Everything had changed.

"Jim," she said, gently. "Your father told me before we got engaged all about his hatred for Wilfred Fisher. He told me all the bad things he did. He told me he had been consumed with hatred and it was a terrible thing. He wanted me to know that about him. And he wanted me to know that he was ashamed of it. Said he wanted to dedicate his life to loving what there was to love and turning the other cheek to what he could not love. Those were his words. We even said them in our wedding vows."

Jim rubbed his eyes with his fingers. "I'm sorry," he muttered.

"I accept your apology. That girl has made *you* crazy."

A scratching noise at the outside door stopped them both. Jim was on his feet in an instant. The noise came again. Jim opened the door and Snoot dashed inside, sopping wet. She stopped and arched her back, then lifted a paw sticky with coagulated paint. Jim picked her up. Held onto her squirming wetness. Took a step, felt the soles of his shoes stick to the floor.

Iris stood up with a sigh. "Sleep," she said. "Nothing more should be said and nothing can be done until we've both had a sleep."

Jim swallowed hard, buried his head in the purring cat. It wasn't true, of course — that nothing could be done before sleep. Before his mother went to sleep she had the livestock to feed. He wanted to help, but didn't have the strength. He kicked off his shoes by the parlour door, submitted to a bone-crunching hug from his mother, then headed towards his room.

Thoroughly defeated, he noticed, passing through the parlour, that his binder was gone. The transcript from the *Expositor*, the photo — everything. And who had taken that?

20

The school bus came and went, its yellow sides and empty windows splattered with muck. Jim heard it pass from somewhere just under the surface of a sleep filled with running and Poochie barking and Fisher shouting and Ruth Rose's eyes filled with hatred.

It was noon when he woke up, his head woozy, his body aching all over. He lay in bed startled by the grey daylight like water wrung from a sponge mop. He wondered where he was. Snoot, beside him, rolled over to have her tummy rubbed. Jim complied.

Before his waking eyes he saw again the look of loathing Ruth Rose had hurled at him when she left.

Betrayal. That's what he had seen, though he had been too enraged to recognize it.

Betrayal? Surely she was the one who had betrayed him. Vandalized his home.

Or had she?

She had the motive. She had the time. But if she had done it, she had not given anything away at Billy Bones' or on the walk home. Was that part of her illness? Could she do something like that and completely forget it had ever happened? Jim had heard of such things, but he couldn't believe it.

So what if she really hadn't done it? But then why

didn't she defend herself when he accused her? She had even flung it in his face. *Hey, Jim, you gotta admit. This is a great idea.* What else had she said? *It's just perfect.* What did that mean?

His mind was working overtime as he pulled on his tatty robe and slippers. He peeked into the spare room. Ruth Rose's bedclothes were all over the place. He picked up her pillow and held it close to his face, sniffing. The pillow was cold, with no lingering smell of roses. No wonder, the window had been wide open all night. The wind had blown her away. He closed it.

In the kitchen, his mother sat at the table, fixing the phone cable. Hub's red toolbox lay open beside a plate of scarcely touched toast. She looked up, but there was only warmed-over comfort in her dark eyes. He wondered if she had slept at all. She looked back down at her work.

"When I've got this done, I'm calling the police, unless you've got a better idea," she said.

"Maybe you could call Hec instead," he said. She looked at him curiously, as if there were more secrets. "It's just a suggestion."

On the counter he found a paper bag from the bakery with three Danish pastries inside. The paper bag was smeared with red paint. There was red paint everywhere.

She reconnected the phone, then called the factory to let them know she wouldn't be coming in that night.

"I'm going into town," she said. "I don't care if I have to spend our last cent, I'm not going to live in this house with this..." She couldn't go on, didn't need to. The kitchen spoke for itself, no less dreadful by noonlight.

Jim tried to keep his voice calm, sensible sounding. "Mom," he said, "this is going to sound weird, but I'm not so sure Ruth Rose did this."

His mother's face screwed up in an expression of disgust.

"Are you out of your mind?"

Jim took a deep breath. "Maybe," he said.

His mother slammed the tools back into the tool box. "So you are suggesting *he* did this?"

"Maybe."

His mother stared at him. "What kind of a...a lunatic would accuse himself of murder in the house of the victim?"

As impossible as it seemed, Jim thought he knew *exactly* what kind of a lunatic.

"Don't you see," he said, urgently now. "He's talked to you about her. He knows that you know that she thinks he murdered Dad. So this graffiti doesn't tell you anything new." Jim gave up. It sounded ridiculous.

"Jim," said his mother. "Think of what you are saying."

"I *am*."

"No, you're not. She's completely bamboozled you. She's...she's kidnapped your mental faculties."

"No, she hasn't."

"Stop!" said Iris, holding up her hand. Her face was flushed. She stood up, slammed shut the steel top of the tool kit. She glared at him. Then she reached for the phone again and punched a number.

"Hec, please," she said, glancing Jim's way.

Hec was out on a call. "It's urgent, Dorothy," said Iris. "Please tell him to call as soon as he gets back." Jim watched as his mother hung up and started to punch in another set of numbers, then hesitated and hung up.

So. No police. Not yet. And he knew why. They'd had enough police a year ago to last them a lifetime.

Jim made to speak, but she held up her hand.

"Save it!" she said.

He took a seat across the table from her. He tried to compose himself for whatever was coming next. He watched her wipe her eyes with her hand, pinch the bridge of her nose. When she opened her eyes they were bloodshot but looked upon him gently nonetheless.

"Jim," she said. "Remember at church when you came back after so long? Remember how people looked at you?" He remembered, all right. "Some of that, Jim, was sympathy for losing your father. But some of it was something else."

Jim cast her a curious look.

"We...a lot of people...were worried about you," she said. "You were not well for quite awhile there. You remember. We weren't sure...what you might do."

Jim bowed his head. "That's all passed," he said. "I told you."

"I know, Jim. Or at least, I thought I did..."

Jim looked at her with dawning awareness. "You think I'm nuts," he said.

His mother shook her head. "I don't know what to think."

"Yes, you do," he said. "You think I've lost it. Like I'm having delusions. Hey, maybe *I* did this," he shouted, holding out his hands to take in the defiled kitchen.

Iris looked distressed. "Talking like that is only making things worse."

Suddenly Jim knew what it must be like to be Ruth Rose. To always be under a cloud of suspicion, to never be accepted at face value. As soon as you knew she was under medication, that she had been institutionalized, you could never be sure. And Father had made sure *everybody* knew that.

Then he recalled something Fisher had said, about Jim being sick, about it running in the family.

"Hey, maybe I'm like Dad," he said.

Iris sighed.

"That's what Fisher said. Last night. I have the same thing Dad has."

"He didn't say that," said Iris furiously.

"How would you know?" said Jim. "You weren't here." Then he dropped his voice. "Or maybe it wasn't Fisher. Maybe my *voices* told me that."

"Jim!" Iris pushed her hair back off her forehead. "This is no time for joking."

"He threatened me. You think that's a joke?"

"Enough!" said Iris.

He was going to argue, but she stopped him with a steely glance. She closed her eyes. Without opening them again, she said, "I'm going to the hardware store. You think you'll be okay here alone?"

Jim thought of something smart-ass to say, but kept it to himself. "I'll be okay," he said. "I can start cleaning up. When Hec phones I'll ask him to come up here."

He watched her closely, wondered whether he had sounded sane enough. She nodded. Smiled. And, without another word, went upstairs to change. She left with only a hug and a promise to hurry back.

She wasn't gone more than a few minutes when Hec called.

"Jimbo?" he said, his voice wound up tight. "I just heard that your mother called, but I'm glad you're there. I was on the verge of calling you."

"You were?"

"I'm out at the Sagittarius Motel. You know, near the 511 turn-off. There's something I want to talk to you about. Tell your mom I can be up there in fifteen minutes."

Seventeen minutes later, Hec's behemoth old Buick splashed into the yard, looking a bit like a tank and sounding like one, too. It was slathered with mud, basted with it. Hector Protector had waded into battle at a terrible fast pace.

Jim was out in the yard in time to hold the door open as the elderly journalist climbed out of his car.

"What's up?"

Hec's eyes were shining. "Things are hopping all over." With a hand in the small of Jim's back he started to propel him, grandfatherly fashion, towards the house, but Jim stopped in his tracks.

"You'd better tell me out here," Jim said.

Hec looked towards the house, but he didn't push for an explanation.

"Where's Iris?"

"She'll be back in an hour or so." Hec's bushy eyebrows came together in a frown. "What was it you wanted to talk to me about?" Jim added hurriedly.

It was clear that Hec was full of news, but he looked at Jim a moment, the way he might look at a blank page before starting to write a story.

"I'm a newspaperman, born and bred, and I've come to believe that there isn't any such thing as a coincidence." He paused and Jim wondered if he was supposed to say something. But Hec was only composing his story. "When you were in the *Expositor* office a couple of weeks back, you were looking up the fire that took the life of the Tufts lad."

"Francis."

"Right. Now, what would you say if I told you Stanley Tufts was in the neighbourhood?"

"His brother."

"None other," said Hec. "I picked up a call on the police band first thing this morning about some trouble at the Sagittarius Motel, and the trouble had to do with Stanley Tufts."

"But they moved," said Jim. "Down south."

Hec nodded. "The address in the motel registry was Baton Rouge, Louisiana."

"What kind of trouble?" asked Jim.

Hec stuck his hands in his pants pockets. "Trashed his room and took off. Except he didn't take off in his own car. His rental was still sitting right out front. And he left all his stuff behind at the scene of the crime." Hec paused for dramatic effect. "Including some blood."

Jim shook his head in wonderment. It didn't sound like the kind of thing that happened in Ladybank.

"I found myself contemplating," said Hec, "whether you might be able to shed some light on why Stanley Tufts was around here a few weeks after you looked up that story?"

Jim stared off for a moment, his head buzzing. "I don't know," he said. He scratched his head. "Maybe."

Hec took off his glasses and cleaned them with the end of his tie. He put them back on his nose and squinted at Jim. Jim grabbed him by the cuff of his sports jacket and led him towards the kitchen.

Hec stood, amazed, on the threshold. "What in God's sweet name is this all about?" he murmured.

So Jim led him outside to where the kitchen table now stood on the lawn, sat him down on a chair and, as best he could, told him what had happened. He tried to stick to the facts, but whenever he got off track, Hec was quick to steer him back on course, in a manner that embarrassed and somehow reassured Jim at the same time.

When Jim was done, Hec looked at him for a long time, as if the boy were some rare specimen of beetle and Hec was a scientist trying to figure out what genus he belonged to.

"Stanley Tufts, blackmailer?" he said at long last. He didn't roll his eyes, but Jim felt suddenly like a child playing at make-believe.

"Maybe he saw something the night of the fire," said Jim. But Hec shook his head.

"They'd already moved down to Brockville," he said. "I went back and read the report in the *Ex* myself. Stanley would have been...oh, ten or so. Doubt he was up this way alone."

"Yes, sir," said Jim, dropping his head to hide the blush of embarrassment. Then he remembered something else, something that was fact. "Fisher, last night. He looked like he'd been in a fight."

Now Hec looked plainly distrustful. Jim quickly realized his mistake. "I mean, I don't know if it was a fight, but he had a cut on his face, right here." He painted a line along his right cheekbone. "And the collar of his coat was kind of wet with something and there were scratches on his neck. And he didn't have his cross on, the one he always wears."

At this Hec looked genuinely interested. He put his hands on his splayed knees, thumbs out, and leaned forward.

"A crucifix, you mean?"

"Yes, sir."

"What did this crucifix look like?" Jim described it. Hec pondered something for a moment, looking out over the sopping lawn. "Mind if I use your phone?" he asked.

Jim followed him inside and stood at a respectful distance, but not so far that he couldn't hear what Hec was saying.

Hec was phoning the police. Chief Lorne Braithewaite had been the rookie cop who had arrested Francis for arson back in '67, Jim recalled, and it was Constable Braithewaite who had been the first at the site of the fire in '72. Another coincidence, but not a big one in such a small town.

"He's not in? Still up at the scene, eh? No, that's all right. I'll catch up with him."

Hec hung up. He took one last sad look at the graffiti that defiled the kitchen and shook his head. Jim walked him out to the car.

"You stay around, Jimbo," he said. "I've a feeling the chief will want to talk to you real soon." Hec patted his hand and wheeled out of the yard.

Jim was already at work in the kitchen when his mother arrived home. He had unscrewed some shelves, taken down the curtains, removed whatever he could. He went to meet Iris in the yard to help her carry her purchases. Among other things, she had rented a floor sander.

They set to work. Jim let the job at hand claim his whole attention. His mother didn't look like she wanted to talk. Cleaning seemed to be what she had in mind.

Together, they manhandled the fridge and the stove into the parlour. Then she put on a pair of ear-protectors and flipped on the sander. She had only been at it for five minutes when Jim cupped his hands and shouted at her to stop.

The phone was ringing. It was Hec. Ruth Rose had been arrested.

21

Jim listened to Hec without a word, mechanically nodding his head. He thanked him, his voice listless, barely audible.

Then, as Hec was hanging up, Jim thought of something he wanted to say.

"Did she ask after me? I mean, did she want to see me or anything?"

No, she hadn't. Jim grimaced. Then he hung up and stared at his mother for a moment before he could bring himself to explain. He spoke in a flat monotone.

"She broke into the Blessed T. some time this morning. She was painting slogans all over the walls. The same ones as here. Dickie Patterhew caught her, called the cops." Iris shook her head sadly. Jim glared at her. "Don't say it, okay?"

She came and gave him a hug, but he jerked away. "You think Dickie could have held her if she didn't want to get arrested?" he said. His mother didn't answer.

"Where is she now?" she asked.

"They've got her over at the jail until they can figure out what to do with her." Even before Jim had finished the statement, his eyes flashed with panic. "Cripes!" he said, and he punched in the phone number at the *Expositor* again. Dorothy put him through to Hec.

"Hec, it's me," said Jim. "You've got to tell them not to let Father Fisher take her. Not let him *near* her." His mother protested, but Jim turned away and cupped the phone protectively so that she couldn't take it from him. She stood nearby, her arms folded, frowning. He hardly noticed; he was too busy listening to what Hec had to say.

Finally, he hung up again.

"Jim," his mother said, "Father is her legal guardian."

"That's what Hec said, but it doesn't matter anyway. They can't find him. He's not at home. Dickie says he hasn't been at the church. He was supposed to speak at some luncheon in Smiths Falls and he never showed up."

"Maybe he's doing his rounds — the hospital, the nursing homes?"

Jim raised an eyebrow. "They checked everywhere. He's gone."

The two of them stood for a moment in a kind of combative silence. Fisher's disappearance meant only one thing to Jim. He was on the run. His eyes challenged his mother to say different.

Ultimately, she gave up the staring match, put her ear protectors back on and continued to sand the floor. Jim had been washing the walls in preparation for painting, but he abandoned the task and headed outside. He sat at the table in the garden and tried to imagine Ruth Rose in a cell down at the lock-up behind the court. He imagined her shaking the bars and screaming at the guards. You couldn't cage someone like Ruth Rose. What would they do with her? He didn't want to think about it.

Hey, Jim, you've got to admit. This is a great idea.

What if it wasn't an admission, but a declaration? Maybe she hadn't spray-painted their kitchen. Maybe she just liked the idea enough to borrow it. Was that what she had meant?

Jim walked out into the yard past the old pickup, pounding the grimy cab with his fist as he passed. The sound of the sander was lost to him as he headed across the Twelfth Line, picking his way through the puddles.

Finally he stood on the edge of the road in waist-high goldenrod and dried-up Queen Anne's lace. Late September had rusted the greenness but tinted everything lavender with wild aster.

He stared northeast up towards the ridge.

Back in the house he marched straight through the kitchen and the parlour to the little room his mother used as an office. There was a sign on the door that read, Action Central, but it was just a cubbyhole of a room, a place where Iris paid bills and kept seed catalogues.

The survey map lay open on the old roll-top desk where he had left it the other day when he had been searching for Mount Tabor. Now he followed his finger until he found the little black square that represented his own house, pushed on up from there to Purvis Poole's sand and gravel pit and from there worked his way up to the ridge. The contour rings grew closer and closer together with numbers 575, 625, 675 to the highest point of land for miles around, 725. Seven hundred and twenty-five whats? Feet, yards, metres? He didn't know. But high. And there was a little crossed pickaxe and spade that represented a mine with the word "abandoned" written beside it. There were other mine markers, all abandoned, but none so close, none so handy.

He hadn't mentioned Mount Tabor to Hec. His story was unbelievable enough without dragging Biblical references into it. But he remembered what Ruth Rose had said about the ridge that very morning.

"Now we're getting somewhere," he muttered.

He looked up suddenly. His mother was leaning against the door jamb. He hadn't even heard the sander stop. She was frowning. Mercifully, it wasn't a my-son-is-going-crazy kind of frown. More like a there's-work-to-be-done-and-you're-goofing-off kind of a frown. He threw down the map and jumped to his feet.

"Sorry," he said, saluting her as he passed. The last thing he needed now was to have his mother on his case.

They worked hard. Physical labour was not new to either of them but there was more at stake than a job to do. It was like getting back in the saddle when you've been thrown, parachuting again after a risky fall. As he painted, Jim thought of the bright red Coke can he had picked up in the back field only a few weeks earlier, how upset it had made him to know that anyone had been walking around on their land. Who would have thought it would come to this?

Once the sanding was finished, they worked in companionable silence. His mother turned on the local country music station but declared it too bouncy. She turned on CBC-2 for classical music, turned it off when the news came on.

By six, they had a first coat of paint on the walls. Jim had peeled the primer paint off the fridge easily enough, and Iris had taken a hand-sander to the table out on the lawn. Apart from the odd splash and smear, the kitchen looked more or less like home again. They planned on giving the walls a second coat that evening, and, if everything went all right, Iris hoped she might even get a first coat of urethane on the floor by bedtime.

"It's going to look better than ever," she declared as they cleaned up for supper. She could bounce back, find the good in a bad thing. But Jim wondered if he could. There was no use trying to convince anyone that Ruth Rose was a good thing. He needed proof and he was going to get it.

Refreshed by the effort, Iris surprised Jim by suggesting they pick up a pizza. They never ordered take-out. For one thing, they weren't all that near anywhere. For another, they simply didn't have the money for extras.

"Pepperoni *and* sausage," said Jim. Iris made a face as if he were driving a hard bargain.

She made the call — pretended she wanted anchovies, just to watch Jim squirm. They were too far in the boonies to have pizza delivered, but Attila the Hungry, down on Highway 7, was less than twenty minutes away. She set off with a tootle of the horn, and Jim waved and headed back to the house.

It was already getting dark, turning cooler. The wind was picking up, jostling the sky around. He breathed out paint fumes, took in a great big lungful of camomile-scented evening.

He hadn't reached the porch before he heard the sound of an approaching vehicle, a big red, white and blue FedEx van. It was creeping along.

Then, to Jim's surprise, it turned into their yard. He went over expecting to give directions.

"Hawkins?" the man asked. Jim nodded. "Thank God," said the man, waving an imaginary flag in the air in weary triumph. "I been drivin' around these back roads for near forty-five minutes looking for you." He hopped out of the van with a package addressed to Iris Hawkins.

"She's not here," said Jim.

"But she's coming back, right?" said the man, look-ing panicky. "She didn't move away or nothin'?"

"Yes, sir," said Jim. "I mean, no. She'll be back."

"You her secretary?"

Jim smiled. "Sure," he said.

It was all the courier needed to hear. He thrust a clipboard at Jim and showed him where to sign his name. He handed him the package — a shiny plastic FedEx envelope. Then he tipped his hat.

"Pleased to do business with you," he said. "I was afraid I wouldn't get home in time for my son's grad-uation."

Jim scrinched up his face. "Fall convocation isn't for weeks," he said.

The man winked at him. "Boy, my son is only three." Laughing heartily, he jumped back into the van and wheeled out of the yard the way he had come, but a lot faster.

Jim looked the package over, stared at the return address. It was from Nancy Fisher. By the time he reached the house, he knew he was going to open it.

The stepladder stood alone in the centre of the kitchen. Jim perched on it and tore open the envelope. Inside he found two sheets of cream-coloured sta-tionery written on both sides in purple ink. There were flowers around the border. Forget-me-nots. The letter was signed, "Yours most truly, Nancy," and dated the previous day. Attached to it with a purple paper clip was a business-sized envelope, torn open, but with a letter folded inside. The stamp was American, the return address Baton Rouge. The letter was addressed to Father Fisher.

With his heart pounding, Jim read Nancy's note first.

My Dear Iris;
I have always thought of you as a good and kind and brave person.

I am not brave. It has been very hard to bring myself to do what I am doing. I hope you will not think ill of me for intruding on your life or adding to the misery you have already suffered.

The letter attached was written to Father, as you will see. I cannot face the consequences of what it reveals. I am running away. You will think me a feeble and stupid woman, to be passing the buck. I just don't know where to turn! Believe me, it took all my courage to even do this much.

I have tried so hard to believe that the enclosed letter is just a mean and evil lie. I have sat many times by the telephone about to call the author of this letter, but I could not bring myself to do it.

But I cannot go on like this. I am afraid all the time now. May God be with you for taking in Ruth Rose. She is such a difficult soul. Life has never been easy for her. She needed me and I failed her. Please let her know that I love her very much and that I pray we can be reunited someday, God willing.

Yours most truly,
Nancy

Jim could scarcely breathe. He laid Nancy's letter aside on the step of the ladder, carefully, as if it were an explosive device. He opened the envelope. It was typed on off-white bond in lowercase letters. The message was not long.

fisher:
that does it, scumbag. as if thirty-five thou could buy back my son. hawkins has already paid up the hard way. are we happy? no. it isn't what we wanted. we want justice and we'll get it. your time is up.

laverne roncelier

Jim placed the letter on the step but his hand was shaking so badly it fluttered to the newly sanded floor. He picked it up, brushed off the wood dust, read it again, placed it carefully beside the companion letter.

He whimpered. It was just as Ruth Rose had said. But it was worse. Way worse. His father reduced like that to "hawkins." The glorious hub of his life whose disappearance had almost killed him and yet was not enough to satisfy the blood thirst of Tuffy's mother.

They had been in it together. They had killed Tuffy.

He leaned his face against the cool metal rail of the ladder. If this was the truth, he didn't want anything to do with it. He hated Ruth Rose for dragging him down into this. He hated Nancy. He hated Fisher. He hated Laverne Roncelier and Stanley and Francis Tufts — hated him for dying. And he hated his father, too, for leaving him alone to handle all this.

He clung to the ladder and closed his eyes. But a sound — a short, sharp metallic *click-slide-click* — brought him reeling back to the present.

At the door stood Father Fisher with a rifle in his hands. He had just engaged the bolt action to put a shell into the firing chamber. The rifle was aimed at Jim.

22

Fisher was smiling. "My, but the Lord does go on answering my prayers," he said. "That's the power of faith, Jim Hawkins."

Jim knew the rifle. It was a Cooie bolt action .22. It usually sat in a rack above the door in the back room. It was for varmints — raccoons with a taste for the hen house, groundhogs who set up shop in the vegetable garden, beavers that couldn't be persuaded to build elsewhere.

Jim stared at Father Fisher defiantly. Fisher raised the rifle to his shoulder, expertly looking down the sights.

"I grew up in the country, Jim. I know how to use this thing." Jim flinched. It was enough to make Fisher lower the firearm to rest in the crook of his arm. But he didn't engage the safety.

He glanced around the half-painted room. "What a difference a day makes," he said.

"You did it, didn't you?"

Fisher held Jim's angry gaze as if it were a wasp in a jar. "If that's what you care to believe."

"It's what's *true*."

"It's what you *believe* to be true, Jimbo. That doesn't quite make it the Gospel Truth."

"Don't talk to me about the Gospel," said Jim. "You've got red paint all over your hands."

Fisher glanced at the fingers of his hand, unperturbed. "Who's to say it isn't blood?"

"You killed my father," shouted Jim.

Fisher showed no emotion. "Only a lunatic would think to say such a thing." He spoke softly. "Start spreading it around and people just might think you're as crazy as Ruth Rose."

"You killed Francis Tufts," said Jim. "And you killed my father because he was going to tell on you."

"Really?" said Fisher placidly. "You must tell me all about it. Sometime. But right now, I'm on a tight schedule." His eyes wandered again to the letters.

"If this is what you came for, take it," rasped Jim. He threw the letters, which fluttered to the floor in front of the pastor.

Fisher kneeled to retrieve the little bundle. "Thank you," he said. "It would have been far better had I found it last night," he added wearily.

"Ruth Rose didn't have it," said Jim.

Fisher was reading the letter from Laverne, his gaze darting back and forth from the page to his captor.

"I know," he said. "When I didn't have any luck here, I put two and two together and went home again." He folded up the letters and put them in the back pocket of his jeans. He was wearing a denim jacket over a work shirt. He wasn't wearing his dog collar. Jim couldn't recall ever seeing him without it. On his feet were sneakers, wet and speckled with greyish grit. Jim had never seen him dressed in normal clothes.

"Nancy was gone, of course, but I was able to reconstruct her treachery," he said. His eyes invited Jim to ask him how and it gave Jim a certain amount of pleasure not to. But Fisher could not resist a captive audience.

"I found a discarded piece of note paper in the garbage can: an 800 number — FedEx, as it turned out — with the confirmation number jotted down underneath. Handy thing, a confirmation number. That's how I was able to trace the parcel and find that it would be delivered here by three o'clock today." He laughed at this. "Only three hours late," he said. "I have had to wait with the patience of Job."

He had been around the farm somewhere all afternoon. Jim shuddered.

"I must admit," continued Fisher, "I wasn't quite sure how I would handle it. I thought maybe I could cut the courier off at the pass, before you or your mother noticed — what with all the noise and all. I didn't fancy a run-in with Iris. I'm sure you've been telling her all kinds of wild and fanciful stories. I trusted in the Lord to make my way easier. And voilà! Off goes Iris on some errand." He looked at his watch. "It's too early for work, I guess, but there's nowhere she could be going that would take less than half an hour, so here we are, Jim, alone at the end of the world."

The menace in his voice was studied, calculated to frighten. This time Jim didn't flinch. But he had to stop himself from spitting in the man's face. Fisher grinned.

"You hate me, don't you," he said. "Go on, admit it." Jim clenched his fists and swallowed the venom that was filling his mouth.

"Hate will do you in, Jimbo," said the pastor. "Just like it did your father."

Jim launched himself at the man — hurled himself with a vengeance, pushing off from the ladder, which crashed to the floor behind him. His head met Fisher square in the chest, his arms swinging. Fisher gave, but only a little, and the next moment Jim was lying on his back on the floor with the muzzle of the rifle pressed painfully against his chest. He laid his head back, breathing hard, his nose sucking in the burned smell of fine sawdust.

"Hate warps a man, Jim," said Fisher. "Makes him putty in the Devil's hands. It killed Francis Tufts, too. You want to hear the story?"

"No," said Jim. Carefully, he pushed the barrel of the rifle away from his chest. Fisher didn't stop him. His eyes were blazing.

"Your father started the fire that killed Francis Tufts. Bet you didn't know that! No, of course not. Well, it's true. He thought he was burning down my father's hay mow. But he was too full of hate to know or care what the consequences of his action might be. See how it happens? When you're burning up with hate, it doesn't take much."

Fisher's eyes were watering, though his voice remained more or less composed. Jim closed his own eyes, tried to control his breathing. Then he smelled, suddenly, the acrid stink of sweat near his face and opened his eyes to find Fisher kneeling over him, his face so close that Jim had to turn away from the stench.

"After the fire I was scared," said Fisher. "I ran off and hid. Hid and prayed. And that's when the miracle happened. The Lord came into my heart and took up permanent residence there. He decided there was a lot of life in me and it would be a shame to waste it. I did some fierce praying and it *saved our hides*, Jimbo. But did your daddy accept that gift from above? No. He couldn't. Didn't have the faith. And when Stanley and his impertinent mother crawled out of the woodwork a year or so back, Hub got to hating again. Hating *him-*

self. As if he hadn't learned from that fire what hatred can do to a man. He couldn't stop himself, couldn't stand it anymore. You hear what I'm saying, boy?"

Jim lay perfectly still, his head pressed to the floor.

"My trust in the Lord never faltered," said Fisher. "I led Hub to that cabin New Year's Eve. I knew I was a sinner for my part in the whole thing, but I knew the Lord loved me anyway. 'Hated the sin, loved the sinner,' as we like to say. 'Hub,' I told him. 'The Lord knows of our sins. No one else *needs* to. One day we will answer to Him. In the meantime, let's get on with this life the best way we know how.' But could I convince him of that? No, I could not."

Fisher leaned back on his haunches. He lay the rifle across his thighs, looked thoughtful. His face was drawn, his eyes tired.

Then, abruptly, he was back in the present, looking at his watch, climbing to his feet.

"Fifteen minutes," he said. "Wherever your mother got to, she's probably on her way home now." He climbed to his feet. "Which means I should be on my way."

Startled, Jim could only lie perfectly still and watch the man recover the FedEx package from the floor and shove it in his pocket. He looked around to see if there were any other signs of his being there. Satisfied, he turned to Jim.

"Tell your mother I was here, will you? Hmmm, I wonder what she'll say?" Fisher raised his finger to his chin in a caricature of deep reflection.

"Maybe something like, 'Poor Jim. He's having delusions. Only a year ago he was speechless with grief, suicidal. Now he's mad as a hatter. Hooking up with Ruth Rose was the last straw. It was like hooking up with a runaway roller-coaster.'" He tapped his finger on his head. "Go ahead, spill the beans. See where it gets you. But, Jim, please, when you do, don't forget the part about your daddy lighting the match. Tell the *whole* truth now, as you were taught to do. That is, if the truth is what you're after."

Jim stared at Fisher as if he were an alien — something from another planet.

"Of course, I'll refute anything you say," said Fisher. "I'll shake my head sadly and pray for your over-imaginative broken heart. My record, Jim, my goodly deeds, my excess of faith and charity — these things speak so much louder than anything a confused and frightened child might say."

Jim cleared his throat. "What did you do to Stanley?"

Fisher smiled. "Ah, Stanley? He's all right. He'll be gone in a day or two, his tail between his legs, scurrying back to his mother's skirts. I've turned the tables on them, Jim. If Laverne Roncelier wants to see number-two son again, she'll drop her foolish crusade." He sighed. "And then we can all get back to doing the work God put us on earth to do."

"To kill people?"

Fisher's face contorted, with pain, anger — Jim wasn't sure. Then he recovered. "Things happen in this life, Jim. You make a mistake, you ask for the Lord's forgiveness. You move on."

Then he left.

Jim was too stunned to move. He lay there listening to the night, the frogs, a dog barking. He didn't hear a car start up. Fisher must have come on foot. He did hear a train loudly announcing its passage down Ruth Rose Way. In another quarter hour or so, she would hear it herself, rumbling through Ladybank. He imagined her lying in her cell on a cot as hard as any floor, wondering where that train was heading.

He struggled to his feet, his legs wobbly under him. Gently, he touched the back of his head. There would be a bruise on his skull where Fisher had hurled him to the floor. He pulled up his shirt and found a circular impression the diameter of a .22 calibre rifle muzzle. These wounds were the only proof the man had been there.

Were they enough?

Oh, by the way, Mom, while you were out, Father Fisher dropped by. At gunpoint, he stole the blackmail letter Nancy couriered to us. He told me about how Dad killed Francis Tufts twenty-five years ago, but he admitted that he had a part in it. Then he said goodbye and walked off into the night. See, here is the proof.

He thought of the courier. Jim had signed for Nancy's package. Wasn't that proof? Yes, but only proof that a package had arrived. Not proof of what happened to it.

He picked up the ladder, leaned against it. His head was reeling. Ruth Rose was under arrest, Stanley Tufts was being held for ransom, somewhere, until Laverne dropped her accusations. There was no proof of anything.

They could contact Nancy but would she talk? She was obviously scared out of her mind.

The stolen rifle would end up in the bottom of a quarry — or worse — the police would probably find it hidden in Ruth Rose's bedroom. Jim had been wrong. Fisher wasn't on the run; Fisher wasn't even breaking into much of a sweat.

Jim got himself a drink of orange juice from the fridge, closed his eyes and let the sweet coldness revive him. He let his mind wander into the future as far as next Sunday.

Fisher at church.

If everything worked out the way the pastor planned, he would be in church as usual. He would deliver a sermon about the evils of hatred, perhaps — just to taunt Jim. And there was nothing Jim could do to stop him. He could stand up and yell at him. He could write his story out on the walls. Then he'd be carted off like Ruth Rose, with Fisher falling to his knees to pray for his lost soul.

No. Jim could say and do nothing. That was the way the world worked.

In a kind of daze, Jim washed his face with cold water, well water from the stone heart of the earth. He dried himself off. Then, with shaking hands, he gathered some things for supper — plates, cutlery, napkins, glasses — and carried them out to the parlour where the kitchen table now stood. He laid the table and he thought about his father.

His father had done something terrible and he had been ashamed of it. It wasn't hate that killed him, it was shame. But Fisher had no shame and there was no one in the world to bring shame upon him.

Unless...

An idea began to take form in Jim's brain. The hurt faded. The rage faded. His hatred faded. There was no room for it if he was to make his plan work. He had to put aside the past, make his way lightly and carefully through the present and keep his mind on the future. If he could just keep his cool until tomorrow.

Leaning his head against the window, he watched his mother arrive. By the time she entered the house, he had summoned up a smile.

23

Jim had never skipped school before. But then, he had never tried to visit someone in jail, either, or cooked up a plan to track a murderer. It was a day of nevers. A day he would never forget.

He wrote a letter to Ruth Rose on the school bus. The writing was jerky but the message was clear enough. Anyway, he was hoping she would never see it. He was hoping she would see him in person. He imagined a room like in a movie, the two of them sitting on either side of a glass wall with guards at the door in case anybody tried anything funny.

By the time the bus pulled into the school driveway, he knew he wasn't going to be able to wait until lunch time to see her. By lunch time, he might chicken out.

The jail was an historic building attached to the back of the old courthouse on St. James Hill just a few blocks from the library. He had stared up at the high grey walls and barred windows and imagined dark corridors and grizzled, desperate men in striped pyjamas. It was hard to picture Ruth Rose in such a place. And it was his fault she was there. She had wanted to be caught because he had let her down.

Inside the front door there was a stiflingly small reception area, bare of any furnishings or decoration. There were three doors and one window with thick glass — bullet-proof glass, Jim suspected — which looked into an office. There was only one person in the office. She wasn't in uniform.

"Can I help you?" she asked, with a look that suggested she couldn't.

Jim bent down to the little talk hole in the glass. "I'd like to speak to one of your prisoners," he said.

The woman behind the glass twitched away a smile. "Did you have a particular one in mind?"

"Ruth Rose Fisher," he said. "I'm not sure if it's visiting hours yet, ma'am, but it's really urgent."

The woman's expression softened. "Well, I'm sorry, but you just missed her. She's gone."

Jim's eyes grew wide with surprise. "She got away?"

The woman nodded vigorously. "Uh-huh. Flew the coop. Some guy came in here with a birthday cake for her and I guess it must have had a rat-tail file hidden in it."

Jim Hawkins the idiot.

"I was just pulling your leg," said the woman good-naturedly. "Ruth Rose was remanded into custody pending her trial."

"What does that mean?"

"Well, she's been charged with public mischief, but we're not going to keep her locked up for that. Usually she'd be out under the supervision of a family member. In this case, no one seemed to be available and Children's Aid wasn't interested. Luckily, someone stepped forward to act as her guardian."

"Not her real guardian?"

"Well, it's a bit unusual," said the woman, leaning on the counter behind the glass. "But Chief Braithewaite figured it was all right. Anyway, the girl was all for it."

"May I ask who took her?" said Jim as politely as possible.

The woman observed Jim closely. He tried to keep eye contact with her, tried not to look like a criminal — hoped she wouldn't ask him why he wasn't in school.

"I guess it can't hurt," she said at last. "She left here with Mr. Menzies, the publisher over at the *Expositor*. How does that sound to you?"

"Great," he said. "Thank you. Thank you very much."

"Now, don't you go getting her in trouble," said the woman. This time, Jim knew enough to smile.

He went directly to the newspaper office. Hec wasn't in. He wasn't at home, either.

"He could be anywhere," said Dorothy.

There was nothing he could do but go back to school. He signed in late and told the secretary he would bring a letter from his mother the next day. It was difficult getting through the day, and the bus ride home seemed to take forever. Then, when he got home, there was no news. No word from Hec, no word from Ruth Rose. What was going on?

Jim tried to help, but his mother shooed him out of the house. "Why don't you go check on those beavers," she said. "Blow off some steam."

He didn't feel like going down to the south pasture, but he did go outside. And then he realized where he really wanted to go.

He set off north across the Twelfth Line. He climbed the split-rail fence and headed towards the ridge, towards Old Tabor.

Fisher was in hiding and he was obviously nearby. That was the only explanation for him being on foot the night before. Jim's bet was on Tabor. And if Jim was right, Tabor was the very place Ruth Rose would make for. He could only hope she would tell Hec Menzies about their suspicions. It was hard to imagine her confiding in anyone after what had happened, but just maybe, if Hec told her what he had told Jim, she would open up. And then, with any luck, Hec would have told Braithewaite and there would be a whole search party already up on the ridge.

That's what Jim hoped to find, anyway.

The field he crossed belonged to Lar Perkins. It was lying fallow this year, the bare earth hard under foot despite the rains. There had been a stiff wind and the going was relatively dry. Jim climbed the sloping field, crossed a rise and fell out of sight of his mother or anyone travelling on the Twelfth that brisk, late afternoon.

He hopped another fence. Now he was on Purvis Poole's property, a sea of tangled weeds. He slogged on a way until he came to the shore of a sea of dunes, the edge of the first sand pit. He jumped down and cut across the pit, his feet sinking into the soggy sand. He had put on his work boots for the climb ahead but they seemed clunky now, and he wished he had worn his sneakers.

Crawling on all fours up the steep northern slope of the pit, he came out on hardpack, a road of sorts, though overgrown and unused. But as he walked, his spirit quickened, for he could see from the broken and leaning grass that something — a vehicle of some kind — had passed through recently.

He tramped past Poole's boarded-up house, climbed another hill, forded another sand pit. He climbed out at another distant shore. He was putting continents between himself and his home. He reached, at last, the place where the rolling meadowland met the bush. He stopped to catch his breath. He turned to look at the valley below, saw the grass bend under the wind.

He could see for miles — Ormond and Pat McCoy's spread to the east, Lar and Charlotte Perkins' land to the west, his own house tucked nicely into the maples below. If he shielded his eyes against the westering sun, he could even make out Highway 7 to the south and the tall towers of the calcite factory on the outskirts of Ladybank.

He turned to face the road ahead, which stretched steeply before him. It was a narrow gash through the trees, mostly bedrock. Fists of granite stuck up through the earth like ancient buried giants trying to fight their way out into the air. The bush closed in on both sides.

In a few minutes Jim's legs ached from the climb, but if he looked at the low juniper growing in the nooks and crannies of the roadway, he saw broken branches and bruised clusters of berries where the chassis of something had passed over. He trod lightly, kept his breath a secret between himself and the air.

He reached a clearing, a flat plateau stretching in low steps up towards the ridge, which was blocked from his vantage point by dense foliage. Crouching on the edge of the clearing, Jim looked for signs of life. The wind swooped down from the ridge, soughing through the pines, shaking the poplars, bending the saplings.

Suddenly, Jim saw a flash — the glitter of light on metal where there shouldn't have been any.

It was a car. Not the Godmobile, but a green four-by-four hidden among the trees on the other side of the clearing. No low-sprung city car could have made it up such a rocky incline.

Jim watched for signs of movement, saw none. He settled on one knee behind a fringe of high grass, yellow and dry, looking as if autumn had wrung the life right out of it.

The four-by-four was a late model Ford Explorer, clean and, to Jim's eye, vaguely official looking. Department of Natural Resources, maybe?

There might be something written on the door. He decided to find out.

As patiently and soundlessly as he could, Jim made his way north around the edge of the clearing. Under the canopy of trees it was cooler and still wet from the rain of the past few days. He was shivering a bit by the time he came to a track, open to the sky but dense with waist-high sumac, its leaves rust-red. The track curved up the hill to his left and disappeared around a bend, heading in the direction of the summit. The ridge loomed above Jim through the waving trees. To his right the track curved down towards where the four-by-four must be parked, though it was hidden from view now by a shoulder of land.

He waited. Watched. Listened. The wind snatched away the blue jays' songs, rattled the crows, whistled out of tune through some hollow place Jim could not see. He ventured on all fours into the sumac and poked his head up like a turtle above the red surface of leaves. Northwest a bit, he saw a caved-in shed of some kind. The door opened and slammed shut again, tugged at by gravity one minute and the wind the next, as if there were a stream of ghosts coming and going.

Jim headed south down the track towards the Ford.

He tripped and only just managed to keep his balance. He tripped again, and this time his knee landed hard on steel, on a rusted stretch of rail. He was following some kind of narrow railbed. He came upon the remains of a broken trolley car lying on its side, its metal chassis frozen with rust, its wooden box rotten and moss-covered. Must have been used to transport ore from the mine, he guessed.

Keeping low but lifting his feet high, he caught sight, at last, of the four-by-four below. There was no insignia on the door. But he was close enough and alone enough, as far as he could tell, to risk taking a peek inside.

There was a break in the trees that seemed to be the course of a dried-up stream bed. The rails crossed the stony bed on a bridge of stout, rough-hewn timbers and the stream bed formed a kind of rocky staircase down towards the clearing. Jim sidled down, step by step, through the dappled light until he arrived, at last, at the vehicle. He stared through his own reflection into the interior, saw nothing at first glance. It seemed show-room clean.

He peered more closely. This time he noticed a dark stain on the back seat, a tiny tear in the upholstery revealing a tuft of stuffing. Then he looked again into the front.

Lying on the plush leather of the passenger seat was a small white cylinder. Lip balm.

He heard a tiny avalanche of gravel and instantly dropped to the ground. Someone was coming from the direction of the cliff. On his stomach, he slithered around the vehicle to the other side. The steps were distant and not in any hurry by the sound of it, but they were unmistakably coming closer.

He looked around. To his left, the ground fell away gently down through a small stretch of open woodland and low ground cover towards the clearing. The clearing was a sprint away. He could probably not escape unseen, but if he could get out into the open he had a good chance. If it was Fisher, Jim was sure he could outrun him if he had a decent head start.

He took another quick look and made up his mind. With a deep breath, he pushed himself off and, keeping low, dashed down through the woods. He had the advantage of surprise. With any luck he would not be observed until he had made the clearing, and then it was all downhill. No one could catch him.

He hadn't counted on the rubble. With lightning reflexes, he cleared the skeletal remains of some kind of steam pump, overgrown and half submerged in the forest floor. He stumbled over a rotted ladder, regained his balance, kept moving.

He never saw the fly wheel.

It was wooden spoked, as large as a cafeteria table and choked by carrion flower. One moment Jim was in full stride, the next he felt a searing pain in his ankle and he was falling. The last thing he saw was clumps of bluish berries in a putrid-smelling sea of dying vines. The last thing he heard were footsteps thundering in his ears.

24

The footsteps came closer, echoing in his head as if his head was empty of anything but footsteps. He should do something. Get up. Run. But his arms wouldn't move, nor would his feet. If he could only stand, that would be a start. So, blindly, he stood and then he keeled over onto his knees.

Strong hands grabbed him by the arms, lifted him, placed him back on a seat, where he fell backwards until he was leaning against stone, cold and wet. He opened his eyes.

Everywhere was stone, even the face before him. Then it became flesh, a man, his features indistinguishable, the only light coming from behind him, a bright halo of light that pricked at Jim's eyes painfully.

The man stepped back a bit and Jim could see now that he had no halo. It was Father Fisher. The next minute he was kneeling before Jim. He had a thermos in one hand and a cup in the other. There was water in the cup. Jim saw the light glimmer on the clear surface of the water. Fisher brought the cup to Jim's lips and he drank.

For a moment, cool water was all there was in the world. Jim leaned back again, breathing hard. He rested. Leaned forward and the cup was there again. He wanted to hold it but for some reason he couldn't. Then it dawned on him that his hands were bound behind him. He felt the rope tight against his wrists. His ankles, too. He started to panic but didn't have the energy for it. He relaxed, opened his eyes, careful not to look into the light.

Fisher's face, what he could see of it, looked worried. His raven hair was mussed, the bruise on his cheek was livid. But then Jim's attention was diverted, for behind Fisher's left shoulder there was another man. He was sitting in what looked like a car seat. Except the car seat wasn't in a car. Where were they?

A cave.

Jim looked up. The walls rose around him, pale as flesh but veined with shining green stones. The same green as Father's crucifix. But he wasn't wearing it now.

And the other man. He was nearer the light and his hair gleamed white — white as corn silk. It was long, tied back in a ponytail. He was looking at Jim, the light glinting off pale blue eyes.

"Tuffy?" said Jim. The man looked pained and that's when Jim noticed that he was tied up as well.

Fisher's hand came towards Jim's face. Jim flinched, but the huge hand only touched his forehead. It felt cool and Jim closed his eyes and leaned against it. With his eyes shut it could almost have been his own father's hand.

"You're all right," said Fisher soothingly. "You had a bad fall."

Jim opened his eyes and squinted at the light that lit the cave. It was a hurricane lamp, kerosene, hanging from a bracket on the wall, a spike jammed into a cleft in the rock. It lit up the top of a large wooden spool, the kind they rolled telephone cable onto. But now it was on its side like a low table.

There was other makeshift furniture: a crate, a shelf made of boards and piled stones, the car seat where the man who was not Tuffy sat.

Jim stared at his fellow captive. He had a ratty sleeping bag draped around his shoulders. His face was cut and bruised. And it came to Jim who it must be. Stanley.

But now Fisher turned Jim's face towards him. "I didn't want it to be like this," he said. "It would all have worked out just fine." The sincerity in his voice seemed so real. He was apologizing. "You shouldn't have come here, Jim," he said. And, unlike the threats of the night before, there was real sadness in his voice. Jim dared to speak.

"What are you going to do?"

Fisher lowered his head. "I don't know," he said. "I just don't know anymore." Then there was silence.

Jim heard water dripping a long way off. It was impossible to tell how big the cavern was, for the lantern only lit up one small corner. Jim looked at the makeshift shelf beside him. There was an old peanut tin filled with odds and ends: a yo-yo, a chrome lighter. Beside the tin, a pile of soggy dime comics, a coiled length of string, a cigar box, a black phone with a dial.

It was a clubhouse. His father, Eldon Fisher and Tuffy had come here, made this place their own. And, looking at Fisher now — still kneeling on the cold floor, his head still bent — Jim knew that it was to this underground room that Fisher had fled the night of the fire that killed Francis Tufts. It was here that God spoke to him, just like in the Sunday school picture.

Except that Fisher had got it wrong. This far underground, it wasn't likely God who had spoken to him.

The parson sighed, took a deep breath and climbed slowly to his feet. He leaned forward, his hands on his knees, the better to look Jim in the eye. "I have to go up top again," he said. "There's a call I'm waiting for."

Jim's eyes skittered to the black telephone, but it wasn't connected to anywhere. He watched Fisher check on Stanley, check the ropes that bound him to his car seat.

"You okay?" Fisher asked.

"Oh, I'm just hunky dory," said Stanley. "Thank you so much for asking." His accent was southern, his tone dry. With one last aggrieved backward glance, Fisher headed off into the gloom beyond the lantern's light. Jim heard his footsteps retreat, following the smaller beam of a pocket flashlight that finally disappeared around some bend in the deeper darkness of the cavern.

"You're Stanley," said Jim.

The man managed a painful smile. "At your service," he said. "Well, truth to tell, *not* at your service."

"Where's he going?"

"Up top," said Stanley. "The four-by-four has a cell phone in it. He borrowed it from some parishioner. Wonder if she has any idea what he wanted it for." Stanley shook his head sadly. "He's waiting for a call from the warden of the church to say a certain package has arrived. In it are some letters from my mother. When he's got them in his hot little hands, then I get released. That's the plan, anyway." He glanced with some exasperation at Jim, but his voice was ironic. "Who are you, anyhow? What you want to do getting yourself in this mess?"

"I'm Jim Hawkins. Hub's son." The good-natured frown on Stanley's face tightened. "I'm sorry for what my father did," said Jim, squaring his chin. "But he couldn't have known he was doing it. My father would have never hurt someone on purpose." His voice was shaking, but there was a kind of cracked pride in it.

Stanley nodded slowly. "I know it," he said. "Fisher tricked him."

"You know what happened?"

Stanley sighed. "Well, according to our talkative captor, Francis came around to Wilf Fisher's house on that New Year's Eve back in '72, wanting money, wanting revenge, even. I don't doubt it. He'd been in that reform school. I suppose he figured it was time he collected. Fisher senior was out. Our holy friend here took my brother in, fed him Christmas leftovers, gave him his father's finest rye — Francis was always partial to drink. Fisher promised him his reward and, when he was good and sleepy, he found him sleeping gear and led him down to our old homestead in the low field. Made sure he was warm and cosy."

He paused to make sure Jim was following.

"Then I guess he went and roused Hub. There was a New Year's gathering at your place as well. Hub snuck out without anyone knowing it. And that's when Fisher tricked him. He complained about his old man, how Wilf, with all his money, kept him on a short chain, what a crab he was, etcetera, etcetera. He kinda threw Hub a bone, you see, and Hub, he gnawed on it. He hated Wilf Fisher and Fisher encouraged him to a white-hot hatred."

Stanley stared off into space for a moment. Jim didn't need to hear the rest. "So he convinced my dad it would be a cool prank to burn down the old house."

Stanley nodded. He turned to Jim. "He lit his fuse, you might say." He paused again in silent reverie. "Dry hay goes up real good," he added. "It must have been quite a blaze."

Jim felt a calmness come over him. This was the whole of the sad truth. His own father was neither guiltless nor entirely guilty. He was the victim of a terrible trick, but also the victim of his own anger. There was no denying it.

Stanley suddenly interrupted his thoughts. "You know what that devil Fisher believes, Jim Hawkins? He believes God sent that mighty snowstorm to cover their tracks. He truly believes the Lord loves him." Stanley stretched the word love, made it two syllables long, a white snowstorm of Love. "I'm not a religious man myself, but that strikes me as the worst kind of blasphemy."

It was perverted. What there was left of faith in Jim was filled with revulsion.

Stanley looked at Jim, and his battered face was a snarl of emotions: anger, remorse, bewilderment. "My mother and I — we kinda blew it, big time." He appealed to Jim with his eyes. "I never wanted to do it at all. Not that I'm pleading innocence here. It was Mother's plan. She had this wicked bee and it wasn't in her bonnet, no, sir, but in her very soul. She had lost her son. She demanded justice. Can you see that?"

"I think so," said Jim. More hate, he was thinking. Hatred begat hatred. "But why so many years after it happened?"

Stanley looked up. "It started with a letter. About two years ago. From an old-timer by the name of Jock Boomhower, a former neighbour of yours, I guess."

Jim nodded. "He wrote a kind of death-bed confession. He went out of his way to track us down, even hired a detective. Then he wrote to us. Told us he'd seen Fisher and your father at the old house the night of the fire. He didn't say nothing at the inquiry. He was mad as hell at Francis. Glad to see him go. So he kept his mouth shut. But I guess he didn't want St. Peter to bring it up when he was standing at the heavenly gates, if you catch my meaning."

Jim nodded. "Why'd Boomhower hate Francis?"

Stanley shook his head. "Because Francis, God rest his soul, was an idiot. They were all idiots, the three of them, and I don't mind telling you that. But it was my brother — without a doubt the biggest idiot of the lot — who took it upon himself to burn down an old shed on Jock Boomhower's spread. 'Cept he didn't know Jock had moved a cow and her new calf in there. Jock didn't get them out. Anyway, Francis was arrested the same night. The others, I guess, were plum terrified. They hadn't been with him that night, but it was enough to make them quit their arsonous ways forever."

"Almost," said Jim.

"Huh?"

"Almost quit forever."

Silence descended again. Jim didn't want to hear any more. He wanted out of the chain of events that had led him here. Out of everything. He wanted to return to the present. He wanted to return to the place where the future started.

He wriggled his wrists tentatively. There was no give. He wriggled his ankles. It was impossible.

"He's good at knots, huh," said Stanley. "A regular boy scout."

Jim tried again until his wrists were chafed and burning.

Stanley didn't watch. "Good luck," he said, dispiritedly. "I been trying for as long as I've been down this God-forsaken hole."

Jim looked around the cavern for something sharp, saw nothing. The lantern flickered, caught his attention. They had lanterns just like that at home. When you lived in the farthest corner of the county, power outages were common, and it took hydro crews a long time to replace fallen lines. Jim knew all about hurricane lanterns.

"I think I've got an idea," he said.

25

Jim stood up. With two hops he made it past the shelf made of boards and piled stones to the cable spool. He sat down and shimmied around until he was facing the crate. He put his bound feet up against the crate and shoved.

It was heavy. It barely moved. But it could be moved. He rocked back, pressing his knuckles into the pitted surface of the spool, leaned his shoulder into the wall, getting as much leverage as he could, and shoved hard with his bound feet. The crate slid with a racket that echoed all around them. It now rested more or less under the lantern. It would have to do.

Jim stood up, lost his balance, sat down again. He needed his arms for balance but they were as securely out of commission as his legs. He tried again, getting up cautiously. He made it. He stood there, trying not to think too much, concentrating on not falling over. He felt light-headed. He took a tentative hop. Another. He teetered a bit but managed to recover.

Some of his confidence regained now, he bent his knees and took a bigger hop. It was a mistake. He began to keel over and it was all he could do to make sure he fell against the crate rather than flat on his face.

"This is quite a show," said Stanley. Jim was lying

face down on the crate. He turned his head to see Stanley grinning wanly at him. It cheered him on.

Flipping himself over and using the wall for support, he wormed his way up onto the top of the crate. It seemed to be able to support his weight. Slowly, he manoeuvred himself into a kneeling position. It took several attempts. He didn't want to make too violent a move for fear of dislodging the top of the crate.

When at last he was on his knees, he needed to take another break. He was already breathing hard and the hardest part was still to come. He sat back on his heels. His wrists and ankles were raw from rope burns, but at least the blood was pumping through his veins.

Leaning back on his toes, Jim hoisted himself up onto his feet. He wobbled and for one terrible moment felt sure he was going to pitch forward to the cave floor, but he managed to tip the other way against the wall. The top of the crate held, though he felt it buckle a little. It might not hold up for long.

"I don't know what you're up to, but you are some kind of kid," said Stanley.

Jim glowed a little brighter. And something happened inside him. It was Hub. Hub way-to-going him as he sawed a plank clean and straight, drove a roofing nail home in two good whacks, made something fit, did something right.

The belly of the lantern was now directly in front of him. The reflection of his face was distorted on its brass surface. As he leaned towards it, he felt the heat of it on his cheeks, his forehead. It was almost comforting in the chill dampness, but he was going to have to get uncomfortably close if he was to do what he planned.

He moved in, sliding his shoulder along the wall until he could take the wire handle of the lantern in his mouth. The handle was already very warm. It would be all right at the top, which is where you would hold it if you were carrying it in your hand, but Jim couldn't reach that high so he had to grab it from the side, where the handle attached to the body of the lamp. He bared his teeth to avoid burning his lips. His cheek was right up against the kerosene reservoir. Sweat poured from his face. His eyes were dazzled by the closeness of the flame. He closed them, bit down hard on the handle, stretched his neck as high as he could and slid the lamp off the spike.

There was no time to lose. He could feel the heat beginning to burn his face. He fell to his knees, leaned forward and placed the lantern on the crate. When he was sure it was stable, he let go and pulled his face away, groaning, breathing the cool air in huge gulps.

"Good on you, son," whispered Stanley.

Jim rested his cheek against the cold stone. He didn't dare stop now. He didn't dare think too much about what he still had to do. He kneeled again, bent over and grasped with his teeth the lever that raised the glass chimney. He raised it and locked it in place.

Then, with his teeth, he turned the brass knob that raised the wick. The brass burned him and he pulled away. He kissed the wall to kill the pain. It tasted sour but deeply cold. He repeated everything. Turn the knob, kiss the wall, turn the knob, kiss the wall. The flame shot higher and higher and straight up, for there was no wind to make it flicker.

Now Jim manoeuvred himself around until his feet were again on the ground and the lantern was behind his back. Gritting his teeth, he held his bound wrists up to the open flame. He craned his neck but he couldn't see what he was doing. He stared at Stanley sitting directly across from him. He pushed his arms out behind him as far as he could. He burned the back of his hand and stifled a howl of pain.

He tried again, bending forward this time so that his shirt didn't catch on fire. With his eyes clamped shut, he screwed up his courage. Knowing what was going to happen next, but beyond caring, he thrust his wrists right into the flame.

He smelled something burning. It might have been the rope, it might have been his skin, but he only pressed harder.

He grimaced and then he howled, no longer caring if anyone heard him.

"Holy Jesus!" he whimpered, gritting his teeth.

"Hang in there, boy!" cried Stanley. "You're almost there!"

And then, suddenly, Jim knew it was working. Even through the pain he could feel the pressure of the rope lessening. He forced his wrists apart. Yes! It was giving. Just another few seconds. Another. The smell of hemp filled the air. It was on fire. He pulled his wrists away from the lantern and the flame followed him. He waved his hands around behind his back pulling at the ropes, feeling them give, pulling some more until finally they let go.

The flaming rope fell to the crate, writhing like a snake in a death agony. Jim brushed it onto the floor and then he rubbed his hands and wrists and arms against the front of his shirt. He glimpsed melting flesh and almost passed out. But he thought of his father — "You can do it, podner" — and made himself go on.

The firey rope went out. He squatted on the floor,

leaned against the wall, pressing his hands palm down against the coldness of stone.

Releasing his ankles was almost as hard. His hands hurt terribly. His fingers were numb and useless against Fisher's knots. But he persevered and, after several agonizing moments stood up, a free man.

He went to Stanley.

"No," said Stanley, shaking his head. "You get yourself outa here and go for help."

Jim ignored him and started in on the man's bound wrists.

"It'll take too long," said Stanley. "Fisher could be back any minute." He smelled horrible and he was shivering badly. Up close Jim could feel how feverish he was.

Jim worked with a passion. Worked with rage. He needed Stanley.

"Look," said Stanley, dropping his voice to a whisper. "The way he left just now is the way he brought me here. It was treacherous — past a deep pit, along a ledge down a cut so narrow and low I thought he was walking me into my own grave. But that isn't how he brought you here."

Jim looked up at him, alert.

"He carried you in over his shoulder. There was no way he could have done that the way he brought me. Besides, look around you. This car seat, the cable spool — this stuff didn't get here the way I did. You can bet on it."

At that moment Jim pulled the rope free from Stanley's wrists. Sick and weary as the man was, he immediately bent to the task of undoing the rest of his ropes while Jim sat back on the cavern floor cradling his burned hands in his shirt, rocking back and forth as if his hands were a baby. He was trying not to faint from the pain.

"Hurry," said Stanley. "Take the lantern. Go! This here stope has another way in, I'm sure of it. Ten to one it's an easier way."

"But —"

"No buts. Wave to me with the lantern when you find it. I don't need eyes to tug on these ropes. Just move. I'll catch you up. You're our only hope."

Jim clambered to his feet. Behind him the lantern on the crate started to flicker. They both looked towards it. Raising the wick had used up fuel far too quickly.

"Get out of here," said Stanley.

The light flickered lower still and Jim didn't wait. He lowered the chimney back into place, then quickly trimmed the wick to preserve what fuel there was left.

"Git!" shouted Stanley.

Grabbing the lantern, Jim set out. He found a tunnel soon enough. He hesitated on the threshold. There might be any number of exits. The ceiling was low — what if it petered out altogether? The thought terrified him. But he gathered together his courage, waved the lantern shakily at the dim figure of Stanley, who waved back, and entered the tunnel.

He hurried along now, taking encouragement from the fact that the floor seemed to be heading upwards. The way grew steeper and steeper. He slipped more than once.

Then, suddenly, he saw a break in the darkness ahead and, simultaneously, he smelled a change in the air.

Autumn. He smelled autumn! Earth and rotting leaves. It was the most excruciatingly beautiful aroma he had ever experienced. And the darkness — it was speckled with stars, dimly glowing with moonlight. He turned to go and get Stanley — it wasn't far, now that he knew the way. But even as he turned, the lamp flickered and died.

26

The last bit was the hardest. There seemed to have been some kind of a cave-in at the mouth of the tunnel. It was overgrown but the footing was still treacherous, the rock fragments giving way as Jim slipped again and again. On his third attempt he lost the lamp, which clattered down the scree and rolled into the cave below. It was only then that he wondered why he had been holding on to it at all. With two hands free, he was better able to make the climb. It was almost straight up.

Finally, scratched and bleeding, he dragged himself over a threshold of thorns onto the forest floor. He lay there, his cheek pressed against the mossy ground. How sweet it felt, how beautiful was the stirring of the fir trees. He curled up like a baby, holding his burned hands close, holding himself together. He wasn't sure he would ever move again.

Then he thought of Stanley down there in the dark and he climbed shakily to his knees. On all fours he craned his neck, all his senses straining, a cautious animal. He must not get caught again. Adrenaline might get him home, but he had no energy left to face Fisher.

He saw nothing, heard nothing. Nothing human. A whippoorwill. An owl. He stood up.

Where was he?

There was moonlight but the moon itself was nowhere to be seen. It was in its second quarter now — almost full. He scanned the sky. It seemed brightest along the top of the ridge. It had risen in the east, so he must be on the western side, the home side of the ridge. Good. Jim started south, keeping the ridge on his left.

The wind had settled. A fog came down, whisper thin, wet on his face, soaking up the forest before him, soaking up sound. Everywhere was silence. The woods were thick with it. He resisted the urge to run, remembering his fall.

He passed muddy test pits, signs of another dilapidated shed, an overgrown slag heap with the fog settling on it like a huge slow eiderdown.

And then suddenly he was walking through waist-high sumac. In the moonlight refracted through the drifting fog it stretched before him like a placid river through the trees. He knew where he was now.

He made his way as slowly as the fog, wading through the undergrowth that opened before him and closed after him with scarcely a sound. On his left he saw the dim outline of the ridge etched by eerie moon-glow. Wraiths of fog rose from the dark wall of rock like ghostly smoke from a fire that had gone out years ago.

Jim ducked below the surface of the sumac to collect his wits. Fisher could be anywhere.

He listened. Nothing. No, something. A distant train? Cars on the highway? He sat up tall. He heard the sound again. It was definitely coming from the south. Fisher leaving in the four-by-four? He tried to follow the direction of the noise, and that's when he saw the light that was not the moon's. It was low in the trees, lighting up the underside of the canopy, scattered by the fog into an unnatural glimmering. The light was rising, coming his way.

Jim held his breath. A car's engine. He heard the motor whining, watched the dim light grow, reach out into the darkness. It was someone climbing the road that led up to the plateau. It could be Fisher returning from somewhere. But, no. It wasn't just one vehicle. The noise was growing nearer all the time, reverberating up the wooded hillside, loud enough to drown out any noise he might make.

Jim started to push through the sumac at a faster pace, stumbling on the rails, grabbing the slender limbs of the trees to keep himself aloft, frightened that whoever was coming might turn around and go before he could reach them. He could see the shadowy shapes of the cavalcade, twin beams of headlights, and on the lead car, a cherry, spinning round and round. The police!

They were drawing up onto the plateau, and Jim found himself once again at the dried-up stream bed. The four-by-four was still parked, swaddled in a bright gauze of mist. He couldn't tell if Fisher was in it, but he was too wild with excitement to care. He pitched himself down the embankment, falling, slithering on his backside, running, landing in a heap at the bottom.

Meanwhile, the police vehicles had pulled into a semi-circle on the plateau. There were three of them already — more coming. Their headlights were all aimed up at the ridge.

Jim was blinded; he didn't care. He heard doors opening and slamming shut. Shadowy figures emerged and trained spotlights up at the bush. He heard voices.

"Here!" he cried, waving his hands. "Over here."

Immediately, a searchlight swung around looking for him, dazzling him so that he had to cover his eyes from the glare.

"Jim Hawkins? You all right?"

"I'm okay!" he shouted, waving his arms victoriously.

Then suddenly a shadow peeled itself from the trees and blocked out the light. Fisher. Jim swerved around him but not far enough or fast enough. Fisher's arm flew out and a huge hand closed around his burned wrist, yanking him clear off his feet.

Jim howled in pain and crumpled into Fisher's arms. Then he heard his mother call his name and he fought with all his might, yelling at the top of his lungs until Fisher forced his right arm up high between his shoulder blades, and the pain punched the voice right out of him. Fisher's arm closed tightly across his neck.

An amplified voice came out of the translucent wall of fog.

"The area is completely sealed off, Fisher. We don't want any trouble."

Jim felt Fisher's heart pounding against his back. Then he felt the mighty chest expand, heard the pastor clear his throat.

"Lorne? Is that you?" he said, as if he was calling to an old friend.

"You know it is, Fisher"

"*Father* Fisher, Lorne," he said. He actually chuckled, as if the chief were guilty of a lack of respect. "Listen, Lorne," he said smoothly. "I'm sure we can work something out."

"I'm sure we can, too," said the invisible voice over the loud-hailer. "Just as soon as you let the boy go."

Fisher sighed. "Ah, but that's just it. I can't let the boy go. Surely you must see that."

More spotlights blazed from the left and from the right. Jim watched spectral figures fanning out around him. Through slit eyes, he saw them crouching, running, conferring. He heard the unmistakable sound of firearms being prepared for business. Fisher immediately tightened the grip of his forearm across Jim's windpipe.

"The boy and I are friends, Lorne."

"I know that, Father," came the voice over the loud-hailer. "We're all friends here, so let's take 'er good and easy. Have ourselves a talk."

Jim could hardly breathe. He was on the brink of passing out when, all of a sudden, the pressure across his windpipe lessened. Something had distracted Fisher's attention.

Then Jim heard the dog, the cornfield dog, barking somewhere in the woods just off to the west.

"Over here, Poochie!" screamed a girl's voice from below.

"Ruth Rose!" shouted Jim.

Fisher's huge hand, stinking of kerosene, closed over Jim's mouth. But Jim would not be silenced. Knowing Ruth Rose was there gave him a jolt of courage. He shook his head just free enough to bite down hard on the flesh at the base of his captor's thumb. Fisher yowled and withdrew his hand, but Jim wasn't finished. He lifted his right foot high and brought the heel of his work boot down with all his strength on Fisher's foot. Fisher grunted with pain and Jim tore himself away from the man's grasp and rolled out of his reach.

"Stop!" yelled Braithewaite. "Somebody grab her."

Ruth Rose had broken through the police cordon and run to Jim's aid. She reached him before Fisher and stood between the man and the boy, crouching like a wrestler, daring him to come closer. Others followed Ruth Rose but Fisher seemed not even to notice them. Something in his stepdaughter's eyes seemed to bring him up short. Then the cornfield dog burst into the light and went directly to Ruth Rose's side. She held the dog by his collar, and Fisher backed away as if it was a hound of hell.

Fisher retreated up the stream bed, stumbling, falling. Jim lay watching as several armed police swarmed past him.

Suddenly Jim gasped. For one startling instant, Fisher must have stepped into the convergence of all the searchlight beams. His face became radiant, shining. His clothes glowed as if they were made of light — as if beams of light were passing clear through him.

Then, out of the dazzling haze behind him stepped a fog-enshrouded ghost. It was Stanley Tufts, but his long pale hair was loose and wild and the light was trapped in it like a broken halo. His blue eyes were half mad and in his hands he carried a rock the size of a child's head.

Fisher did not see him. He stepped back right into his path, turned, looked up, cringed and covered his head. Stanley brought the rock down, a glancing blow on Fisher's shoulder. But enough to fell him.

27

His mother held him and, somehow, Jim held her and managed to hold onto Ruth Rose at the same time. Then Hec joined in, holding them all. Even the cornfield dog got his licks in before bounding off into the night.

All the hugging put some colour into Ruth Rose's cheeks but she seemed in shock. She watched two attendants carry Fisher on a stretcher to an ambulance, and her wide eyes blinked like someone waking up from a nightmare.

Laverne Roncelier was wanted for questioning but they didn't need to extradite her; she came on her own as fast as she could. And once she had checked up on Stanley in the Great War Memorial Hospital in Ladybank, she turned herself in to the police. But the blackmail letters, which Fisher had been keeping in the old clubhouse in the cave, clearly revealed that money had never been the object of the exercise. Just as Stanley had said, all she had ever wanted was justice.

Fisher's offer of money had not only been the final insult, but also all the proof she needed of his guilt. It didn't go unnoticed by Jim or other folks in the Ladybank area that the amount Fisher offered

Laverne Roncelier to keep her mouth shut roughly coincided with the money he had raised for the Kosovo relief campaign.

Father Fisher had all kinds of things to say. He had a story for anyone who cared to listen, and they varied as the weather did that autumn. He claimed no responsibility for any wrong-doings. But then, other times his mind slipped a gear and he babbled whole scenes of the drama that had led up to the disappearance of Hub Hawkins. It was as if a little voice inside him was trying to break through the walls of denial behind which he had retreated so many years ago.

One rainy November morning, he told a forensic psychiatrist that he had pushed Hub into a deep mine shaft at Tabor just to put him out of his misery. He seemed to believe he had been doing his old friend a favour. He told how he covered his tracks, leaving the car in the cedar grove, walking away in Hub's own shoes, just as Ruth Rose had suspected. The lip balm dispenser had been his only mistake and he had covered that well enough. He was an impressive liar. A pathological liar.

A police team following up on Fisher's confession, discovered the bones, the earthly remains of Hub Hawkins, at the bottom of a shaft deep inside the mine. He could be laid to rest at last.

It was a strange funeral, well attended, including every preacher from every church in Ladybank and the surrounding countryside.

Jim overheard Hec talking to Iris later about the flock of preachers. "They're here to mourn the loss of something more than a good man," he said. Jim wasn't quite sure what he meant, but he saw a grievous sadness in the eyes of the preachers. Father Fisher had been one of them and yet never really one of them at all. For all his good deeds, he had been an imposter, a fake. He had abused his power horribly and in his actions had made a mockery of what was for them a profound and abiding belief.

Ormond McCoy built a pine coffin for the funeral. Pat McCoy and Daisy Tysick helped Iris with the luncheon which was held at the farm. Nancy helped, too. It was hard for her to be there at all, but she returned from Tweed at Iris's request. And at the request of Ruth Rose. It was Ruth Rose who reminded anyone who would listen of her mother's bravery in sending the letters to Iris.

Lettie Kitchen brought her horrible green Jello with miniature marshmallows to the funeral. Hec Menzies went around getting people to try it. "Ever taste anything like that?" he asked in disbelief.

The Church of the Blessed Transfiguration came through with a loan to help out Jim and Iris. Iris had a good mind not to accept it, but Hec was able to convince her that she would be doing *them* a favour if she could accept the donation. The Church had a lot of healing to do.

So Iris was able to quit her job at the soap factory and concentrate on the farm. She and Jim planned crops together on winter evenings. Sometimes Ruth Rose was there. She seemed to live somewhere between her own new home, an apartment on the outskirts of Ladybank that she shared with Nancy, and her adopted home with Jim and Iris. The two households were connected by Ruth Rose Way.

Jim showed her how to do farm chores. She didn't much like farm chores. In the fullness of winter when the land hibernated under a thick goose-down of snow, he taught her to cross-country ski.

One day they followed the lane down through the cornfields to the low land. They passed through the cedar grove, Jim in the lead, carving a path. The grove held no ghosts for him any longer. Ruth Rose followed at a safe distance — she wasn't all that sure on her skis. But as the hill grew steeper, the distance between them grew shorter. She was going too fast — couldn't help it. She was out of control.

"Look out!" she called — too late. Before Jim could get out of her path, she slammed into him, sending him flying head first into the snow. She came tumbling after.

They finally stopped laughing and extricated themselves from the pile of pick-up sticks that were their limbs and poles and skis. Ruth Rose, glad to be on her own two feet again, ploughed through the snow to the beaver dam.

"Look at this," she called excitedly to Jim.

It was Gladys, long forgotten, up to her waist in a snowdrift, but still standing guard over the breech in the dam. Her purple fedora had blown away and was caught in the branches of a nearby tree. Her pink fright-wig was more frightful than ever, embroidered with brown leaves and twigs.

"Poor old thing," said Ruth Rose. "Let's straighten you up."

She groomed the scarecrow's tousled locks while Jim reclaimed her fedora with the help of a ski pole.

"What's this?" Ruth Rose asked. She had found the plastic bag Jim had pinned to Gladys's chest. There was a sheet of water-stained paper inside; the message was no longer decipherable. Jim took the sheet from her.

"It said something like No Beavers or Crazy Girls Allowed."

"I figured as much," said Ruth Rose and shoved him off the beaver dam into a deep drift of snow. Then she turned her attention to the scarecrow. "We can stay if we want, can't we, Gladdy?" She wrapped her arms around the stick figure to give her a hug but pulled away quickly. "Pee-ew!" she said. "You stink, girl." She made a face at Jim, then her eyes lit up. "But I know how to fix that." And, unzipping her parka, she dug from an inner pocket a glass vial half filled with rose water. The vial glittered in the snow-white light.

She opened the bottle and sprinkled a few drops over Gladys. She put a dab or two behind where her ears might have been if she'd had any. She stopped and gazed at the little bottle, smiling at some memory. Then suddenly she tipped it over the scarecrow until the last drop glistening on the glass lip dripped off, soaked up in its ragtag clothes.

Jim closed his eyes, breathed in deeply. It was like bottled spring when the world was still knee-deep in winter.

When he opened his eyes, Ruth Rose was tucking the empty vial into one of Gladys's tuxedo pockets.

They headed back to their skis, but when they were all strapped in and Ruth Rose had already got her skis in the groove for home, Jim said, "I'll catch you up," turned the other way and headed down through the gulch alone.

He crossed Incognito Creek — invisible now, buried, waiting for the melt. Then he slogged up the hill that led to the back meadow. Out in the open, the sun was warm, though the wind was brisk. It felt wonderfully cool on his face, flushed with the exertion of his climb.

He stopped in the middle of the field and looked around. There were fences that needed mending, but nothing a few cedar poles and wire couldn't fix. Ormond had mentioned he had some cedar, if Jim was interested. And once the meadow was secure, they could think about getting in a head or two of beef cattle again. Start slowly, begin to build up a herd. It was good grazing land up here. A shame to waste.

He turned and started heading back towards the house. They could talk about it over supper. The three of them.